All I Want for Christmas is You

TANISHA STEWART

All I Want for Christmas is You

Books may be purchased in quantity and for special sales by contacting the publisher, Tanisha Stewart, at tanishastewart.author@gmail.com.

First Edition
Published in the United States of America
by Tanisha Stewart

Table of Contents

Shout Outs

A special shout out to author Niomie Roland for coming through at the buzzer with feedback that helped elevate this sweet little angel's story lol...

If you are a romance lover, check out her books – her catalog is extensive! Start with her Christmas series: book one is called Until the Snow Melts.

Also, shout out to J.R. Mason for helping with some details to help the story pop. Check out her thriller catalog – start with the How to Kill series.

All I Want for Christmas is You

Chapter 1

Jasmin watched the snowflakes drift lazily through the December air, landing softly on the playground. Her classmates squealed with delight, their breath visible in puffs of white against the winter chill. But Jasmin wasn't interested in their childish excitement. Her mind was elsewhere, calculating, planning.

It had been three months since Daddy moved out. Of Mom crying in the bathroom when she thought Jasmin couldn't hear. Of awkward weekend visits and hushed phone calls. Jasmin hated it.

"Hey, Weirdo."

Jasmin turned to see Sienna Jacobson standing behind her, ruddy-cheeked and smirking. Jasmin didn't respond, just stared with unblinking eyes that made most kids uncomfortable. But Sienna wasn't most kids.

"Did you hear me?" Sienna pressed, stepping closer. "I said, your dad came over to my house last night. For dinner." Her voice dropped to a whisper. "My mom says he might be my new daddy soon. Too bad for you."

Something cold and sharp twisted inside Jasmin's chest. Not anger—something deeper, more precise. She tilted her head, studying Sienna's face as if memorizing it for later.

"We're playing snowball teams," Jasmin said finally, her voice flat. "Want to play?"

Sienna looked surprised by the invitation but nodded. "Sure. I'll be on the winning team, though."

Jasmin smiled. It didn't reach her eyes. "We'll see."

As the children divided into teams and began gathering snow, Jasmin wandered to the edge of the playground where the snow had partially melted, revealing the gravel beneath. She selected a rock—jagged, with one particularly sharp edge—and rolled it between her gloved fingers before packing snow around it with precision.

The perfect snowball.

When the game began, chaos erupted across the playground. Snowballs flew in every direction, children shouting and laughing. Jasmin waited, watching Sienna's red hat bobbing through the crowd.

Three. Two. One.

Jasmin threw with perfect aim, a skill developed during countless hours of solitary practice. The weighted snowball connected with Sienna's forehead with a dull thud that Jasmin could almost feel on her own head.

For a moment, everything seemed to stop. Then Sienna's scream cut through the playground noise as blood began to trickle down her face, bright red against the white snow.

Teachers rushed over. Children gathered in a circle. "Who threw that?" Ms. Peterson demanded, holding a sobbing Sienna.

"I don't know!" Sienna wailed. "There were so many snowballs!" But her eyes zeroed in on Jasmin's cold dark pupils trained on her from across the playground.

The rest of Jasmin's features bore a mask of innocent concern. But as the teachers led Sienna away to the nurse's office, Jasmin's lips curved into a small, satisfied smile.

Phase one complete.

After all, Christmas was coming. And all Jasmin wanted was her family back—no matter what it took.

Chapter 2

Jasmin dropped her backpack by the front door, the weight of the day still heavy on her shoulders. The satisfaction from the playground incident had faded during the long bus ride home, replaced by the familiar emptiness of returning to a house that no longer felt whole.

"Mom?" she called out. No answer.

The smell of charred sugar and burnt dough hit her next. Following the scent toward the kitchen, she paused when she spotted a figure in the living room. Her mother sat motionless on the couch, staring at the muted television, earbuds in her ears and a half-empty beer dangling from her fingertips. Three more empty bottles lined the coffee table.

Something pricked at Jasmin's heart. Not quite sympathy, but recognition. Her mother was broken too, missing the piece of their family that had walked out.

Jasmin approached slowly, waving her hand in front of her mother's vacant eyes.

Her mother blinked rapidly, yanking out an earbud. "Oh, hey baby." Her voice slurred. "I tried to bake you some cookies." A tear slid down her cheek, leaving a faint trail of mascara.

Jasmin reached out, wiping the tear away with her thumb. The gesture wasn't entirely natural—more something she'd seen in movies—but she performed it with precision.

"It's okay, Mommy," she said softly.

Her mother sniffled. "There's a couple that didn't get messed up. They're on the counter."

Jasmin nodded and headed to the kitchen. True to her mother's word, three perfectly golden cookies sat on a cooling rack. The rest had clearly met a different fate—the trash can was filled with blackened discs, burnt beyond recognition.

She poured herself a glass of milk and ran her hand over the surviving cookies. Still warm. She picked one up, dipping it into the cold milk as her mind drifted back to the problem at hand.

How to get her parents back together. How to fix what was broken.

Jasmin's mind traveled back to her parent's last argument. Her father's voice, raised in anger: *"I'm leaving, Malia! I'm never coming back!"* Her mother on her knees, fingers clutching at his sleeve: *"Please, don't do this. We can work it out."*

Jasmin had watched from the shadows of the hallway, unnoticed by either parent. She remembered how still she'd been, like a small predator observing, calculating. Not crying—just watching, learning.

A tear slid down her cheek now, surprising her. She wiped it away quickly, studying the moisture on her fingertip with curiosity. Her perfect family was being torn apart. Her father was with Sienna's mother now. Moving on. Replacing them.

But families were like puzzles. The pieces had to fit together correctly. Her father belonged with her mother. With her.

Jasmin took another bite of cookie, chewing as she considered her next move. The incident with Sienna was just the beginning.

She thought about her father sitting at Sienna's dinner table, laughing with Sienna's mother, perhaps reaching for her hand across the table. The image made something dark stir inside her.

Her perfect family would not be replaced. Not if she could help it.

And Jasmin was very, very helpful.

Chapter 3

Jasmin woke to silence. Usually, her mother would be in the kitchen by now, coffee maker gurgling, radio playing softly in the background. But today, nothing. She dressed quickly in the cold morning air, her breath visible in her bedroom.

The hallway was dark as she approached her mother's door. She knocked softly, hearing a muffled sniffle from the other side.

"Yes, honey?" Malia's voice was thick with emotion.

Jasmin pushed the door open slowly. The room was dark, shades drawn against the morning light, but her mother's face was illuminated by the blue glow of her phone screen. Her eyes were puffy, red-rimmed.

"I'm heading to school," Jasmin said, studying her mother carefully.

Malia nodded, attempting to smile. She quickly lowered her phone, but not before Jasmin caught the gesture.

"What were you doing?" Jasmin asked, nodding toward the phone.

"Nothing," Malia said, straightening her posture. A terrible liar. "Just thinking about your Daddy."

Jasmin froze, mind racing through possibilities before settling on the most likely answer. Her father had updated his relationship status last night. She'd seen it herself through the burner account she'd created on her secret phone: a cheap model purchased with saved allowance money. The new profile picture showed him smiling with Sienna's mother, arms wrapped around each other, looking like they belonged together.

Being in fifth grade, Jasmin's parents had deemed her too young for a cell phone. But Jasmin had long ago learned that rules were merely suggestions to be circumvented when necessary. Many things in her life operated this way—there was a lot her parents didn't know about her. The secret phone. The fake accounts. The quiet hours spent researching things no ten-year-old should know.

She'd table those thoughts for now.

"Have a good day," Jasmin said, injecting her voice with a sweetness she'd practiced in her bathroom mirror. Like activating a machine, her mother's lips lifted into a small smile.

"You too, baby."

Jasmin nodded and left, grabbing her backpack from her bedroom before heading out to the bus stop. The morning air bit at her cheeks as she waited, watching her breath form clouds in front of her face.

On the bus, she took her usual seat alone by the window. The other children knew to leave her be—an unspoken agreement formed years ago. Online, she was different. In games, she could be whoever she wanted, make friends, manipulate situations. But here, in the real world, isolation suited her purposes better.

As the bus pulled up to the school, Jasmin spotted a familiar car in the drop-off lane. Sienna's mother's silver SUV. She watched carefully as the car door opened and Sienna emerged, the bandage on her forehead clearly visible even from this distance.

A small smile played at the corners of Jasmin's lips. Her handiwork.

As Jasmin stepped off the bus, she caught Sienna's mother looking in her direction. Without hesitation, Jasmin smiled softly and offered a friendly wave. The woman looked startled, then returned the gesture uncertainly.

Keep your friends close and enemies closer. That's what people said, wasn't it? Jasmin didn't have many friends—didn't particularly want them—but she knew exactly who her enemies were.

Sienna and her mother were trying to steal what was hers.

As Jasmin walked toward the school entrance, her mind was already formulating the next step in her plan. The snowball had been a warning shot. But clearly, more drastic measures would be required.

Christmas was coming. And Jasmin knew exactly what she wanted under the tree.

Chapter 4

The classroom was warm after the winter chill outside, filled with the scent of chalk dust and the faint sweetness of the hand sanitizer Mrs. Watson insisted everyone use upon entry. Jasmin had just settled her backpack on the floor when she felt Sienna's presence beside her, leaning in close.

"I know it was you, with the snowball," Sienna whispered, her breath hot against Jasmin's ear.

Jasmin widened her eyes, adopting an expression of shock at her words. "Why would you—"

"But just you wait," Sienna cut her off, voice barely audible. "I've got something for you."

Something flickered inside Jasmin—not fear, but a spark of excitement. A thrill. What exactly could Sienna have planned? Whatever it was, it would be amateur hour compared to what Jasmin could devise. The possibilities were already blooming in her mind.

"I don't know what you're talking about," Jasmin responded, attempting to sound frightened. Instead, her voice came out taunting, almost playful.

Sienna's lips curved into a smirk, as if she believed she had the upper hand. "Just you wait."

They locked eyes for several seconds, a silent challenge passing between them before Sienna broke away first, sliding into her assigned seat. Jasmin took her own seat directly behind Sienna, completely unbothered. In fact, she was looking forward to whatever game Sienna thought they were playing.

Games had winners and losers. And Jasmin never lost.

At the front of the classroom, Mrs. Watson was calling roll, her voice bright with the forced enthusiasm of elementary school teachers everywhere. When finished, she clapped her hands together.

"Today in Social Studies, we're continuing our discussion of early American presidents!"

Jasmin suppressed an eye roll. She couldn't be less interested if she tried. School had always been simple for her—her mind absorbed information efficiently when she wanted it to, which meant she could spend most lectures thinking about more important matters.

Like how sharp a pencil would need to be to penetrate a human skull. Specifically, the back of Sienna's skull, just a foot away from where Jasmin's hand rested on her desk.

"Jasmin?"

She blinked, suddenly aware that every eye in the classroom was on her, including Mrs. Watson's expectant gaze.

"I'm sorry?" Jasmin asked, her voice the perfect blend of politeness and confusion.

Mrs. Watson smiled patiently. "I asked, who was the third president of the United States?"

Jasmin paused, pretending to search her memory though the answer was immediately available. "Thomas Jefferson?" she said, adding a questioning lilt to her voice.

It worked like a charm. Mrs. Watson's eyes lit up with that familiar teacher's delight at a student's success. "Correct! Great job, Jasmin!"

A snicker came from the seat in front of her. Sienna.

"What's so funny, Sienna?" Mrs. Watson asked, her smile faltering.

Sienna turned in her seat, eyes glittering with malice. "I bet Jasmin can't name the next five presidents after that."

The classroom fell silent. All eyes turned to Jasmin again, but this time with a different energy—the collective anticipation of potential failure.

Mrs. Watson's smile widened, taking the bait. "Well, that would be an excellent challenge! Jasmin, can you name presidents four through nine?"

Jasmin felt heat rising in her cheeks. She had only memorized the first five presidents, a fact Sienna had somehow discovered. How? Had she seen Jasmin's study notes? Had she been watching her?

"The fourth was James Madison," Jasmin began confidently, then faltered. "And then... James Monroe? And... um..."

Snickers rippled through the classroom. Jasmin's hands clenched beneath her desk, fingernails digging half-moons into her palms. Her blood boiled with a quiet rage, but her face remained carefully composed. Only her eyes betrayed her, fixed on the back of Sienna's head with an intensity that might have frightened anyone who noticed.

"That's two correct!" Mrs. Watson said quickly, stepping in to save Jasmin from further embarrassment. "After Monroe came John Quincy Adams, then Andrew Jackson, and John Tyler. Very challenging question, Sienna."

The lesson continued, but Jasmin had mentally checked out. Her mind was consumed with the humiliation, the rage, and most importantly, the planning. Sienna had escalated their quiet war. Public humiliation. A clever move, Jasmin had to admit.

But Sienna would soon learn that she was playing a game with rules she didn't understand, against an opponent who had no limits.

Chapter 5

It was time.

Enough of the school day had passed for everyone, including Sienna, to forget what had been done to Jasmin. But Jasmin would never forget, and when she was finished, neither would her nemesis.

Art class was scheduled to be held between two periods. The first half of the class was held before lunch and recess, and the second half was held afterward.

Perfect timing for what Jasmin had in mind.

"And remember, students," Mrs. Barton said, clapping her hands to get the art class's attention, "these family gifts are special because they come from your heart."

Jasmin watched the art teacher pace between tables, inspecting the various projects in different stages of completion. Christmas was only two weeks away, and the school's annual family gift project was in full swing. Every student was creating something personal for a loved one.

Most kids were making simple items for their parents—clay handprint ornaments, painted photo frames, the usual elementary school fare. But across the room, Sienna was working on something more elaborate.

"My grandmother is turning one hundred years old on Christmas Day," Jasmin had overheard Sienna telling a group of admiring girls earlier that week. "We're having this huge party, and I'm making her something special."

Jasmin observed with calculated interest as Sienna carefully applied delicate brushstrokes to a ceramic music box. She had painted a surprisingly good portrait of her grandmother on the lid, surrounded by a border of tiny roses. The inside of the box, according to Sienna's endless boasting, would play "You Are My Sunshine"—her grandmother's favorite song.

"It's the last one Mrs. Barton had," Sienna had said proudly. "She ordered it specially for me."

Jasmin's project—a lumpy clay bowl for her mother—sat forgotten as she watched Sienna work. An idea began to form, crystallizing with each passing minute.

When the bell rang signaling clean-up time, Jasmin moved quickly. Her paintbrush clattered to the floor, sending red paint splattering everywhere. As expected, several students rushed to help, creating the perfect chaotic moment.

"Oh no!" Jasmin exclaimed, drawing Mrs. Barton's attention. "I'm so sorry!"

"It's alright, dear. Accidents happen." Mrs. Barton hurried over with paper towels.

In the commotion, Jasmin slipped between tables, quickly tucking Sienna's music box into her smock pocket. The weight of it felt satisfying against her hip as she returned to help clean the spill.

Once the cleaning was done, the class quickly filed into a single line so they could hurry to lunch and recess - most students' favorite time of the day.

During lunch, Jasmin slipped out to the bathroom and that was where she planted Sienna's Christmas gift exactly where it needed to be.

Her movements were so precise and stealthy that no one noticed she had disappeared, even her teacher.

When they returned for the second half of art class, it was showtime.

Sienna was among the last to notice her project was missing.

"Mrs. Barton?" Her voice rose in panic. "My music box is gone!"

The teacher frowned. "Are you sure you didn't put it on the drying shelf?"

"No! It was right here! I was just finishing the roses!"

Jasmin watched, fascinated, as Sienna's face reddened and tears formed in her eyes. She began frantically searching under tables, growing increasingly hysterical.

"Someone took it!" Sienna cried, her voice cracking. Suddenly, her eyes locked onto Jasmin. "It was her! She took it!"

The classroom fell silent. Jasmin felt all eyes turn to her.

"Me?" Jasmin's voice quavered perfectly—a practiced tremor. "Why would I take your music box?"

"Because you hate me!" Sienna shouted, advancing toward her. "Ever since you hit me with that snowball—"

"That's enough," Mrs. Barton interrupted, stepping between them. "Sienna, that's a serious accusation. Do you have any proof?"

Sienna pointed a trembling finger. "She's evil! She's trying to ruin everything!"

Jasmin's eyes filled with tears on command—a trick she'd mastered years ago by thinking about puppies dying. "I didn't take anything," she whispered, her lower lip trembling. "Why is she being so mean to me?"

Mrs. Barton wrapped a comforting arm around Jasmin's shoulders. "Sienna, I think you need to calm down. We'll look for your music box. I'm sure it's here somewhere."

"Check her bag!" Sienna demanded, nearly hysterical now.

The teacher sighed but nodded. "Would you mind, Jasmin? Just to clear things up?"

"Okay," Jasmin said softly, handing over her backpack. She knew exactly what they wouldn't find.

The search expanded through the afternoon. Art supplies were moved, shelves checked, even the trash cans emptied. Principal Walker was called in, and the situation escalated when Sienna refused to back down from her accusations.

"Perhaps we should check all the students' lockers," Principal Walker finally suggested, his face grim.

Jasmin had been waiting for this moment. During lunch, while everyone was in the cafeteria, she had slipped the music box into Sienna's own locker, pushing it to the very back behind her winter coat.

The locker search began. Jasmin stood quietly beside Mrs. Barton, the perfect picture of wounded innocence as each metal door was opened and inspected.

When they reached Sienna's locker, Principal Walker pulled out books, folders, and finally the winter coat, revealing the ceramic music box tucked behind it.

The silence was deafening.

"It appears," Principal Walker said slowly, "that you misplaced your own project, Sienna."

Sienna's face drained of color. "No! That's impossible! I didn't put it there! She must have—"

"That's enough!" Mrs. Barton's voice was sharp. "You've caused quite a scene today, young lady. And you've falsely accused a classmate of something very serious."

Tears streamed down Sienna's face, but now they were tears of humiliation rather than anger. "But I didn't—"

"I think you owe Jasmin an apology," Principal Walker said firmly.

Sienna turned to Jasmin, her eyes filled with confusion and hurt. "I'm... I'm sorry," she whispered.

Jasmin nodded, sniffling. "It's okay," she said softly. "Maybe you just forgot."

As the adults turned away, satisfied with the resolution, Sienna's eyes met Jasmin's. Something passed between them. Something Sienna didn't seem to understand at first.

Then, as Sienna watched, Jasmin's lips curved into that small, secret smile.

The smile that said: This is just the beginning.

Chapter 6

The rest of the school day passed pleasantly for Jasmin. She savored the occasional glimpses of Sienna's reddened eyes and hunched shoulders. The music box incident had gone even better than she'd anticipated. Mrs. Barton had given Sienna extra work as punishment for disrupting class with her "false accusations," and the other students had been whispering about it all day.

Perfect victories left a sweet taste, like the cherry lollipop Jasmin now sucked as she packed her backpack at final bell. She took her time, watching as Sienna hurried out ahead of her. Normally, Jasmin would have waited longer to ensure they didn't cross paths, but today she felt invincible.

The December afternoon was already growing dark as Jasmin stepped through the double doors of the school's main entrance. A light snow had begun to fall, dusting the concrete steps with a thin white layer. She paused at the top step, adjusting her scarf against the cold.

She never saw Sienna waiting.

The shove came suddenly—hard hands against her back, propelling her forward with unexpected force. Jasmin's cherry lollipop flew from her mouth as she pitched forward, arms flailing. Her knees hit the concrete first, then her palms, skidding on the light snow and scraping against the rough surface beneath.

Startled but not truly hurt, Jasmin twisted to look up. Sienna stood over her, lips curled into a triumphant sneer.

But something else caught Jasmin's attention: Ms. Peterson, one of the fourth-grade teachers, had just emerged from the building and was staring at them with wide eyes.

In that split second, Jasmin made her decision.

The wail that erupted from her throat was piercing. She curled forward, clutching her knee as her body began to convulse with theatrical sobs. Tears—real ones this time, summoned by a swift bite to the inside of her cheek—streamed down her face.

"My knee!" she screamed, her voice cracking perfectly. "I can't—I can't—" She let herself hyperventilate, chest heaving dramatically.

The effect was instantaneous. Students froze on the walkway, turning to stare. Sienna's sneer faltered, confusion and then alarm replacing her momentary satisfaction.

"What happened here?" Ms. Peterson demanded, rushing down the steps.

Jasmin only cried harder, rocking back and forth now. She'd seen a similar performance in a movie once—a car accident victim with a broken femur. She mimicked it now, adding a high-pitched keening sound that seemed to unnerve everyone around her.

"She pushed me!" Jasmin finally gasped between sobs. "She pushed me down the steps!"

"I didn't—I mean, I did, but—" Sienna stammered, backing away.

Ms. Peterson knelt beside Jasmin, her face etched with concern. "Can you stand, sweetie?"

Jasmin tried, making a show of putting weight on her right leg before collapsing with another cry of pain. "It hurts so bad," she whimpered.

"Sienna!" A sharp voice cut through the gathering crowd. Sienna's mother pushed forward, her face draining of color as she took in the scene. "What did you just do?"

Sienna's mouth opened and closed, no words emerging. She looked trapped, cornered.

Jasmin saw her opportunity and seized it.

"She's been bullying me all day," she sobbed, making eye contact with Sienna's mother. "And this morning, she threatened me!"

Mrs. Watson appeared then, drawn by the commotion. "What's going on?"

"Sienna pushed Jasmin down the steps," Ms. Peterson explained, still supporting Jasmin's weight. "We need to get her to the nurse, and then I think the principal needs to be involved."

"No!" Sienna protested, finding her voice at last. "She's lying! She's been—"

"Enough," her mother hissed, gripping Sienna's arm. "We'll discuss this with the principal."

The next twenty minutes unfolded exactly as Jasmin had hoped. The nurse found nothing seriously wrong with her knee—"Just bruising, thankfully"—but recommended ice and rest. By the time they assembled in Principal

Walker's office, Jasmin was seated with an ice pack, her face tear-streaked but composed.

Her mother arrived shortly after, rushing to her side with genuine concern. "Baby, what happened?"

"Mrs. Reynolds," Principal Walker began, "I'm afraid there's been an incident between Jasmin and Sienna."

The mediation meeting that followed was Jasmin's finest performance yet. She spoke softly, her voice occasionally breaking as she recounted not just the stairs incident, but an entirely fabricated history of Sienna's "bullying."

"She says mean things to me all the time," Jasmin said, eyes downcast. "She told me my dad left because he didn't love me anymore."

Her mother gasped, reaching for her hand. Jasmin saw Sienna's mother shoot her daughter a horrified look.

"I didn't say that!" Sienna protested. "She's making it all up! She's the one who—"

"Sienna," Principal Walker interrupted firmly. "We have a witness who saw you push Jasmin down the stairs. And this comes after you falsely accused her of taking your art project this morning."

Sienna's defense crumbled visibly. She looked from her mother to the principal, then to Jasmin's tear-stained face. Confusion and doubt filled her eyes.

"I... I didn't mean to hurt her," she finally whispered. "I was just so angry about today..."

"That doesn't excuse violence," her mother said, voice tight with disappointment.

What followed was precisely what Jasmin had calculated: Sienna, faced with overwhelming evidence and adult disapproval, began to question her own perception. By the end of the hour-long meeting, she had accepted a three-day suspension and had been made to apologize not just for the pushing, but for the "pattern of bullying" that Jasmin had invented.

"I'm really sorry, Jasmin," Sienna said, her voice small and sincere. "I shouldn't have treated you that way."

Jasmin nodded, accepting the apology with apparent graciousness. "I forgive you," she said softly. "I just want it to stop."

As they left the office, Sienna walked ahead with her mother, shoulders slumped in defeat. At the school entrance, she glanced back at Jasmin—and froze.

For one unguarded moment, Jasmin had allowed herself to savor her victory. The smile that curved her lips was cold, triumphant, unmistakable in its meaning.

Sienna stopped short, causing her mother to look back questioningly. But by then, Jasmin's expression had returned to one of quiet hurt, her eyes downcast, her mother's arm protectively around her shoulders.

They parted ways in the parking lot, each girl entering a different car. As her mother drove past Sienna's car, Jasmin turned her head, meeting Sienna's wide, frightened eyes through the window.

Checkmate.

In the growing darkness, Jasmin finally allowed herself a full smile. Phase one of her plan was proceeding perfectly. Sienna was neutralized—confused, discredited, and afraid.

Now it was time to focus on the adults.

Chapter 7

The evening had settled into a quiet rhythm in the Reynolds household. Jasmin sat cross-legged on her bed, math worksheet spread before her, solving equations with mechanical efficiency. Her thoughts, however, were elsewhere—calculating probabilities of a different sort.

Her bedroom door creaked open. Her mother stood in the doorway, cell phone gripped tightly in her hand. Jasmin noticed immediately how her mother's knuckles had tightened around the device, how her face was carefully arranged into an expressionless mask.

"Your father wants to talk to you," she said, voice flat and lifeless.

Jasmin felt a jolt of excitement but kept her face neutral. She'd learned early that showing too much enthusiasm about her father only hurt her mother more.

"Okay." She set down her pencil and reached for the phone.

Her mother handed it over without making eye contact, then hesitated in the doorway. "I'll be in the kitchen if you need me," she murmured before pulling the door partially closed behind her.

Jasmin waited until her mother's footsteps faded down the hallway before pressing the phone to her ear. "Hello?" she said, injecting reluctance into her tone.

"Hey baby girl!" Her father's voice came through the line, rich with affection.

The sound made something inside Jasmin simultaneously soften and sharpen. David Reynolds had always had that effect on her—he was the only person who could reach past her calculations to something genuine beneath. It made her love him. It made her furious with him.

"Hi Daddy," she replied, unable to keep a small smile from her voice.

"So what happened today?" His tone shifted, becoming more serious.

Jasmin stiffened. "What do you mean?"

"I heard about the incident at school between you and Sienna."

Of course. Shanika would have told him everything, painting her precious daughter as the victim of circumstances. Jasmin considered her options rapidly, evaluating and discarding several approaches before settling on the most effective.

"Daddy, I don't know what to do," she whispered, allowing her voice to tremble. "I'm afraid of her."

"Afraid? Baby, what's going on?"

"Sienna's been saying things to me," Jasmin continued, building the foundation carefully. She felt tears welling—genuine ones this time, summoned by thoughts of her father living with them: Shanika and Sienna. "She... she said you don't love me anymore." Her voice cracked authentically. "She says you are her daddy now!"

"Baby, no," her father said immediately, distress evident in his voice. "That couldn't be further from the truth. You are my one and only baby girl and that will never change."

Jasmin pressed her advantage. "But Sienna will be your new daughter when you marry her mother," she said, the words coming out in a rush, "and you will forget all about me and Mommy."

A heavy silence fell. Jasmin could almost see her father running a hand through his waves, the way he always did when troubled.

"Baby girl, that's not true," he finally said, but his voice had lost some of its certainty.

The silence stretched between them, filled with things unsaid.

"How about this?" her father eventually offered. "How about you come over with me, Sienna, and Shanika? That way you and Sienna can get to know each other outside of school and maybe even be friends."

It was exactly what Jasmin had hoped for—an invitation into the enemy camp.

"But Daddy, she doesn't want to be my friend!" Jasmin protested, her voice rising with hysteria. "She hates me!"

"Calm down, sweetheart," he soothed. "We'll work it out. You two got off on a bad foot, but you'll see that you have a lot in common. I'm sure we can resolve the issue."

Jasmin allowed her breathing to slow gradually, as if his words were comforting her. "You won't leave me alone with her, will you?" she asked in a small voice.

"Absolutely not," her father promised, relief evident in his tone now that she seemed to be coming around. "I'll be right there with you both. You'll see—you two will be best friends in no time, trust me."

The irony almost made Jasmin laugh. Trust wasn't something her father should be offering so freely, not when he had no idea what he was inviting into his new home.

"Okay, Daddy," she said softly. "I'll try. For you."

They made arrangements for Saturday—a casual lunch at the apartment he now shared with Shanika. Jasmin agreed to come over at noon.

"I love you, princess," her father said before hanging up. "More than anything in this world."

"I love you too, Daddy," Jasmin replied, and for once, she didn't have to manufacture the emotion in her voice.

She set the phone down on her bedspread, staring at it for a long moment. She could hear her mother moving around in the kitchen—the sharp clatter of dishes being washed with unnecessary force, cabinet doors closing a little too loudly.

Jasmin moved to her desk and opened her journal. Inside, past the innocuous entries about school and friends that anyone might find if they snooped, was a folded piece of paper. She opened it, revealing a list written in her neat handwriting:

Phase 1: Discredit Sienna ✓

Phase 2: Drive wedge between Dad and Shanika

Phase 3: Bring Daddy home for Christmas

She picked up a pencil and began adding details under Phase 2. Saturday would provide the perfect opportunity to gather intelligence and plant the first seeds of doubt.

Her mother appeared in the doorway again, her face carefully composed. "What did your father want?"

Jasmin looked up, arranging her features into a neutral expression. "He wants me to come over on Saturday. To try to make friends with Sienna."

Something flickered in her mother's eyes—hurt, perhaps, or resignation. "Do you want to go?"

Jasmin nodded slowly. "I think I should."

Her mother's lips pressed together, but she nodded. "If that's what you want."

After her mother left, Jasmin returned to her planning. The invitation was exactly what she needed—access to Shanika's home, to her personal space, to all the vulnerabilities she hadn't yet discovered.

Christmas was just two weeks away. Sienna might think she had allies in this war, but she was wrong. Her mother might believe she had won David Reynolds, but she would soon learn otherwise.

Jasmin smiled to herself as she folded the paper and tucked it away again. It wasn't Sienna who needed to worry about trust now—it was her father. But by the time he figured that out, it would be far too late.

Chapter 8

The chicken was overcooked. Again.

Jasmin poked at the dry meat with her fork, watching as her mother pushed food around her plate without eating much. The silence between them felt heavy, interrupted only by the occasional scrape of utensils against ceramic.

The kitchen still smelled faintly of burned cookies from the day before. Once, her mother had been an excellent cook, taking pride in elaborate family dinners. Now everything seemed to be either overcooked or undercooked, as if her mother's mind was perpetually elsewhere.

Jasmin knew her mother was suffering. The dark circles under her eyes had deepened in recent weeks, and she moved through the house like a ghost, going through the motions of living without actually being present.

Jasmin's fingers tightened around her fork. Part of it was her mother's fault. If she hadn't... She let the thought go. There was no time to dwell on the past. She needed to secure their future. Come hell or high water, she would not allow Sienna to steal her father.

"Are you really afraid of her?"

The question cut through the silence, startling Jasmin out of her thoughts. She looked up to find her mother studying her with an intensity that had been absent for months.

There was something in her mother's eyes—a certain knowing that made Jasmin uneasy. She had to play this right.

"Sienna?" she asked, injecting as much innocence into her voice as possible.

Her mother nodded silently, still watching her.

Jasmin swallowed and nodded reluctantly, as if admitting something difficult. "Yes," she whispered, dropping her gaze to her plate.

The silence stretched between them. Jasmin could feel her mother's eyes on her, searching for something. She maintained her posture of discomfort, not meeting her mother's gaze.

Finally, her mother sighed. "Alright," she said quietly.

Jasmin couldn't tell if her mother believed her or if she had simply decided not to press the issue. Either way, the questioning stopped.

"You can be excused if you're finished," her mother said, rising to clear her own barely-touched meal.

"Thank you," Jasmin said politely, carrying her plate to the sink.

Her mother touched her shoulder briefly as Jasmin passed. The gesture was so unexpected that Jasmin almost flinched.

"Jasmin," her mother said softly, "you know you can talk to me about anything, right? Anything at all."

Something inside Jasmin wavered—a brief, uncomfortable sensation of being seen through. But she quickly steadied herself.

"I know, Mom," she replied with a small smile. "I'm just tired."

Her mother nodded, releasing her. "Get some rest, then. It's been a long day."

In her bedroom, Jasmin went through the motions of preparing for bed. She changed into pajamas, brushed her teeth, and turned off her light promptly at nine o'clock. Then she lay in the darkness, listening to the subtle sounds of the house.

Her mother moved around for another hour—washing dishes, folding laundry, all the mundane tasks that continued regardless of whether her marriage was falling apart. Finally, Jasmin heard her mother's footsteps on the stairs, followed by the soft click of her bedroom door closing.

Jasmin waited another fifteen minutes to be sure. Then she slipped out of bed and knelt on the floor, feeling beneath her bed frame for the loose floorboard. She pried it up and retrieved the phone.

The blue light illuminated her face in the darkness as she activated the gaming app, one of those multiplayer strategy games populated mostly by teenagers and adults. She logged in as DarkQueen10 and joined a public server, pretending to play casually while really watching for one specific username.

Eight minutes later, he appeared: SnakeEyes77.

Her lips curved into a smile as she sent him a private game invitation. They played for a few minutes, their avatars battling across a digital landscape while they exchanged seemingly innocent game-related messages. Then came the question she'd been waiting for.

SnakeEyes77: Did you do it yet?

Jasmin's heart skipped a beat.

DarkQueen10: Yup

SnakeEyes77: How did it go?

DarkQueen10: Even better than we thought. She's suspended for 3 days. And now I'm invited to their apartment on Saturday.

She could almost feel his approval radiating through the screen. Most people would be horrified to know ten-year-old Jasmin was communicating with a 42-year-old man at night from her bedroom. Her parents would be devastated. But they didn't understand what Jasmin understood—that age was irrelevant when two minds connected on a deeper level.

SnakeEyes77 had never been inappropriate with her. He never asked for photos or personal information beyond what she volunteered. He simply listened, understood her in ways no one else did, and offered advice that always seemed to work.

SnakeEyes77: Good. What's next?

DarkQueen10: Saturday is the meeting with them. I need this plan to move quickly. I need to break them up, but it can't be traced back to me. What should I do?

There was a pause, longer than usual. Jasmin waited, watching the three dots that indicated he was typing appear and disappear several times. Finally, a message came through with a devil emoji.

SnakeEyes77: I have just the plan

Jasmin exhaled her relief.

DarkQueen10: Tell me

Chapter 9

Jasmin had to play this carefully. Today was the meeting with Sienna, Shanika, and her father. Shanika had asked what Jasmin's favorite lunch was in an effort to make her feel welcome. Jasmin kept it simple - pizza.

This meeting wasn't about food - it was about gathering information.

Saturday morning arrived with gray skies and a chill that seeped through the windows. Jasmin stood at her bedroom mirror, considering her outfit. Nothing too mature or sophisticated—that would put Shanika on guard. Nothing too childish either—she needed to appear vulnerable but not pathetic.

She settled on jeans, a light pink sweater, and her hair pulled back with a white bobo. The perfect picture of innocent girlhood.

Her mother knocked softly before entering. "Your father just texted. He'll be here in five minutes."

Jasmin nodded, watching her mother's reflection in the mirror. Malia's eyes were tired, but she'd made an effort today—a touch of makeup, her hair neatly styled, a blouse Jasmin recognized as one her father had always complimented.

"Are you sure you want to go?" her mother asked, the same question she'd posed three times already this morning.

"I'm sure, Mom," Jasmin replied, turning to face her. "I need to try."

Her mother nodded, then reached out to adjust Jasmin's ponytail. "Just be yourself, okay?"

Jasmin smiled. If only her mother knew which "self" that truly was.

The doorbell rang, and Jasmin felt a flutter of anticipation. Her mother's hand lingered on her shoulder for a moment before falling away.

"Let's not keep him waiting," she said softly.

Downstairs, her father stood in the entryway, his familiar cologne filling the space. His face broke into a wide smile when he saw Jasmin.

"There's my princess!" David exclaimed, opening his arms.

Jasmin moved into his embrace but made sure to keep her posture rigid, her smile not quite reaching her eyes.

"Hi, Daddy," she said, adding a tremor to her voice.

David pulled back, his brow creased with concern. "Hey now, what's with the long face? This is going to be fun."

"I know," Jasmin said quietly. "I'm just nervous."

David looked past her to where Malia stood on the bottom step, watching them. Their eyes met, and even Jasmin could feel the current that passed between them.

Malia's face softened for just a moment, a flash of longing so powerful it seemed to fill the room. David's Adam's apple bobbed as he swallowed hard.

"Malia," he said, his voice rougher than before. "You look nice."

"Thank you," she replied simply.

The tiny pang in Jasmin's heart surprised her. Though she didn't experience emotion like other people—she never had—she could see the obvious love her parents still shared for one another. All she had to do was make it stick.

"We should go," David said finally, breaking the spell. "Don't want to keep them waiting."

Malia nodded, then bent to kiss Jasmin's cheek. "Call me if you need anything," she whispered.

David guided Jasmin to the car with a hand on her shoulder. Jasmin glanced back to see her mother watching from the doorway, arms crossed as if holding herself together.

Inside the car, her father turned on the radio at low volume—one of those adult contemporary stations that played inoffensive, forgettable music. He pulled away from the curb, casting one last glance at the house in his rearview mirror.

"So," he began in that forced-cheerful tone adults used when trying to disguise tension, "how's school?"

Jasmin tensed. He would know how school was if he was in the home with them where he belonged. But she didn't say this.

Instead, she said, "It's mostly fine. Outside of Sienna."

She faced him squarely, studying his profile as he drove. It was clear her comment made him uncomfortable, but he tried his best to shrug it off.

"Don't worry about that, sweetheart," he said. "You'll see. Shanika and Sienna are both cool."

Jasmin went in for the kill. "Cooler than me and Mommy?"

David's hands tightened on the steering wheel. The silence that followed told Jasmin she had him right where she wanted him. His eyes welled with tears, which pricked her heart unexpectedly, but he quickly blinked them away.

The rest of the drive passed in silence until they pulled up to Shanika's house, which wasn't far from where Jasmin and her mother lived—only a few blocks away. The proximity felt like another betrayal. He had chosen to be this close, yet still apart from them.

David shifted the gear into park and turned to face her.

"Listen, baby girl," he said, his voice low and serious. "You will never be replaced. I love you to the moon and back. You are the light of my world and no one could ever change that. Do you believe me?"

Though her father was clearly sincere, Jasmin couldn't help but push him a little further. "What about Mommy?" she asked, feigning vulnerability. "You're going to replace Mommy. That's not fair."

Her father fell silent again, and once more, Jasmin knew she had won. Her questions were burning him up; she could see it.

Then he delivered the dagger. "Sweetheart, things just didn't work out between me and your mother. But of course I will always love her and wish her the best. And regardless of how we feel about each other, neither of us will ever stop loving you."

That wasn't what Jasmin wanted to hear. He was speaking about her mother in past tense. Rage coiled in her belly, but she couldn't show it. Instead, she nodded slowly, as if processing difficult information.

"Okay," she whispered. "I understand."

David smiled, relieved. "That's my girl. Now let's go have some pizza and a good time, alright?"

As they exited the vehicle, Jasmin spotted Shanika standing on the doorstep, a welcoming smile on her face. She was pretty in that effortless way that some women had—perfectly parted box braids, minimal makeup, a bright yellow sweater that complemented her deep brown skin.

Behind her stood Sienna, looking uncharacteristically shy, eyes downcast. The suspension from school had clearly affected her.

Jasmin fought to keep her features neutral as she followed her father up the walkway. Soon both of them would be in past tense.

Chapter 10

Jasmin studied Shanika's facial expressions, her body language, everything. Time was winding up, and Christmas would be here before she knew it. If she was going to pull this off, everything had to be on point.

"Welcome, Jasmin!" Shanika called, her voice warm. "I'm so glad you could come today."

Jasmin offered a small, hesitant smile. "Thank you for having me," she replied politely.

"The pizza just arrived," Shanika continued, stepping back to let them inside. "I got half cheese, half pepperoni—wasn't sure which you'd prefer."

"Either is fine," Jasmin said, making a mental note of Shanika's considerate approach. It would be harder to turn her father against someone genuinely kind.

The apartment was small but tastefully decorated. Jasmin's eyes moved quickly, cataloging details—family photos showing Sienna at various ages, a bookshelf filled with medical texts (was Shanika in healthcare?), a laptop open on the dining table, three wine glasses drying beside the sink.

As they moved into the living room, David placed a hand on Sienna's shoulder. "Sienna, I believe you have something to say to Jasmin."

Sienna looked up, meeting Jasmin's gaze directly. There was defiance there, but also resignation.

"I'm sorry about what happened at school," she said, her voice flat. "It won't happen again."

Jasmin widened her eyes, the perfect picture of a child trying to be brave. "Thank you," she whispered. "I'm sorry too."

Shanika smiled, clearly relieved. "Well, that's a good start! Why don't we all sit down and enjoy lunch? Afterwards, maybe you girls could play a game or something?"

Jasmin nodded agreeably while noting how Sienna's jaw clenched at the suggestion. This was going to be an interesting afternoon indeed.

As they settled around the dining table, Jasmin kept her posture hunched, her movements careful and measured. She accepted the plate Shanika offered with a murmured "thank you" and took small, neat bites of her pizza.

All the while, her mind was working—observing interactions, noting the way David's hand occasionally brushed Shanika's, cataloging the prescription bottle visible on the kitchen counter (allergy medication?), and watching for any opening that might present itself.

"So, Jasmin," Shanika said warmly, "your dad tells me you're quite the artist. Do you have a favorite thing to draw?"

Jasmin looked up, allowing a genuine smile to touch her lips. "I like drawing people," she said truthfully. What she didn't add was that she particularly enjoyed drawing people in distress.

"That's wonderful," Shanika replied. "Sienna loves art too—don't you, honey? Maybe you two could collaborate sometime."

Sienna's expression made it clear what she thought of that suggestion.

"Maybe," Jasmin agreed softly, while thinking: *Not in this lifetime.*

The conversation continued. Jasmin maintained her shy, nervous demeanor while mentally recording every detail—the way Shanika touched her neck when she laughed, the wine collection visible in the kitchen, the slight tension between Shanika and Sienna that suggested recent arguments.

Most importantly, she watched her father—how his eyes followed Shanika around the room, how his laughter sounded different here than it had at home, how he seemed simultaneously more relaxed and more guarded.

Jasmin took another small bite of pizza, her mind already formulating the next phase of her plan.

They had no idea what was coming.

Chapter 11

As they finished their pizza, David wiped his mouth with a napkin and leaned forward with enthusiasm. "So, I've been thinking," he began, his eyes moving between Jasmin and Sienna. "We should plan something fun that we could all do together. Maybe a day trip or a weekend getaway?"

Shanika smiled encouragingly. "That's a great idea. Girls, any suggestions?"

Sienna, who had been quiet throughout most of lunch, suddenly perked up. "What about Disney World?" she suggested, her voice animated for the first time that day. "We could go during winter break."

"That's not a bad idea," David nodded appreciatively. "Jasmin, you've always loved Disney."

Jasmin offered a half-smile. "It could be fun, as long as that's after Christmas," she agreed softly, making sure to lock eyes with her father when she said *after Christmas*. Then she tilted her head thoughtfully. "Or what about the Statue of Liberty? I've been learning about it in school, and I've never been."

As the words left her mouth, Jasmin's mind filled with vivid images—the four of them climbing the narrow spiral staircase, reaching the crown with its panoramic views of the harbor. In her vision, she saw herself behind Shanika and Sienna, a small push sending them tumbling with screaming voices down to—

Her dark fantasy halted abruptly when Shanika giggled nervously, her hand fluttering to her throat.

Jasmin perked up, curious. "What?" she asked, fighting to keep the intensity of her interest at bay.

Shanika's smile turned sheepish. "Baby girl, that's two of my fears at once. I am petrified of heights and terrified of closed spaces."

David reached over to squeeze Shanika's hand. "Come on, baby, we will all be there togeth—"

"Closed spaces?" Jasmin interrupted, leaning forward. "You're claustrophobic?"

Shanika looked at her in surprise, clearly taken aback by Jasmin's familiarity with the term. "Yes, I sure am," she confirmed. "I've always been that way, ever since childhood."

Jasmin widened her eyes with feigned innocence. "But what closed spaces would there be at the Statue of Liberty?"

Shanika giggled again, though there was tension beneath the sound. "Well, you know, the elevator ride up. I'm sure there will be tons of people and..." her voice trailed off as she fanned herself with her napkin, as if merely envisioning the moment was enough to trigger anxiety. "I just cannot do it."

Jasmin spoke in a solemn yet condescending tone. "My Daddy always tells me that we need to be brave and face our fears."

The table fell silent. David shifted uncomfortably in his chair, caught between his daughter's pointed comment and his girlfriend's obvious discomfort.

From across the table, Jasmin felt Sienna's eyes on her. She met the other girl's gaze and saw the subtle look of disgust there—a look that said Sienna had caught something in Jasmin's tone that the adults had missed. It didn't bother Jasmin. In fact, it was almost amusing how perceptive Sienna was, yet how powerless she was to do anything about it.

David cleared his throat and changed the subject. "So, did I tell you guys about what happened at work yesterday? The VP came in wearing two completely different shoes!"

The tension broke as Shanika laughed gratefully at the anecdote. Sienna smiled politely while Jasmin faked a laugh too, making sure it sounded just childlike enough.

After a few more minutes of small talk, David glanced between the two girls with an expectant look. "Hey, why don't you girls go play in Sienna's room? Get to know each other a little better?"

Jasmin wanted to protest—she wasn't finished gathering information—but it was clear from her father's body language that he and Shanika had planned this play session. Probably wanted some "adult time" to discuss how well the lunch was going.

Sienna awkwardly rose from the table. "Sure," she said flatly. "Come on, Jasmin."

Jasmin reluctantly followed her down the hall, making sure to cast a sidelong glance at her father as she walked, as if uncertain about how this was about to go. The look of reassurance he gave her would have been comforting if she'd actually needed it.

As they moved down the hallway, Jasmin caught snippets of whispered conversation behind them.

"—going better than I expected—"

"—still not sure about—"

The rest faded as Sienna pushed open her bedroom door and gestured for Jasmin to enter.

Chapter 12

The room was exactly what Jasmin would have expected—posters of female athletes on the walls, a desk cluttered with schoolwork, and a bookshelf filled with young adult novels. A framed drawing of Sienna and Shanika sat on the nightstand, confirming Shanika's earlier comment about Sienna's interest in art.

Sienna closed the door halfway and crossed her arms. "So," she said flatly.

Jasmin moved to the edge of the bed and sat down, folding her hands in her lap. "So," she echoed.

"Let's just cut to it," Sienna said, leaning against her desk. "I don't like you, and you don't like me. But our parents are trying to make this work, so we're stuck with each other."

Jasmin blinked up at her with wide eyes. "I never said I don't like you."

Sienna scoffed. "Please. I saw how you looked at me at school. And that comment about facing fears was messed up."

"I was just repeating what my daddy always tells me," Jasmin said, her voice small and defensive.

"Yeah, right." Sienna pushed away from the desk and moved to the window, looking out at the street below.

"Look, I'm sorry about what happened at school. That was wrong, and I shouldn't have done it."

The apology caught Jasmin off guard. It sounded genuine, which was annoying.

"It's okay," Jasmin said, forcing vulnerability into her voice. "Kids at school are always picking on me. I'm used to it."

Sienna turned to look at her, expression skeptical. "Are they? Because from what I've seen, most of them seem to think you're this perfect little angel."

Jasmin allowed her lower lip to tremble. "They're nice to my face because they're afraid of getting in trouble. But they say things behind my back."

For a second, Sienna seemed to waver, as if unsure whether to believe her. Then she shook her head. "Whatever. Let's just get through this afternoon, okay? You stay on your side of the room, I'll stay on mine, and when they call us for dessert or whatever, we'll pretend we had a great time."

Jasmin nodded, the perfect picture of a child accepting unfair treatment. "Okay."

The two girls stared at each other awkwardly for several moments. Sienna sat rigidly on her bed while Jasmin perched on the edge, the silence between them growing heavier by the second. Finally, Sienna sighed and broke the ice.

"Do you like makeup?" she asked, her tone somewhere between reluctant and hopeful.

Jasmin perked up, genuinely intrigued by the unexpected question. "Sure," she replied, though she had never actually considered wearing makeup herself.

"My mom buys me the adult kind," Sienna boasted, a hint of pride entering her voice. "But she says that I can't wear it outside the house. I'm really good at it though. Wanna see?"

Jasmin didn't miss the condescending way Sienna referred to how her mother bought her the "adult kind" of makeup, as if that somehow made Shanika better than Malia. But she pretended to give in, nodding with feigned interest.

"Okay," she said, injecting just enough enthusiasm into her voice to sound convincing.

Sienna's demeanor shifted immediately. She bounced off the bed and moved to her vanity, pulling open drawers and gathering an impressive array of makeup supplies. As she had claimed, she really did have all the adult stuff—expensive-looking palettes, tubes of foundation, mascara, and lipsticks in various shades.

Jasmin stood silently behind Sienna, watching her through the reflection in the vanity mirror as her nemesis settled onto a small stool and began an unrequested makeup tutorial.

"First, you need primer," Sienna explained, her voice taking on a teacherly tone as she dabbed a clear substance onto her blemish-free mahogany colored face. "It helps the makeup stick better and last longer."

She continued to explain each step as if Jasmin was five years old, but Jasmin couldn't help noticing that Sienna actually was good at makeup. Her movements were confident as she applied foundation, concealer, and powder in quick succession.

"See, the key is blending," Sienna said, using a fluffy brush to smooth out the edges. "A lot of girls don't blend enough and end up with those weird lines."

As her face transformed, she began to look beautiful, like a princess from one of those Disney movies her classmates were always talking about. The makeup enhanced her features, making her eyes appear larger, her cheekbones more defined, her lips fuller.

Jasmin watched with a growing sense of irritation. Sienna had always been one of the popular girls at school. One that all the other kids liked and wanted to be around. While Jasmin was often overlooked and ignored, except when she got into mischief.

Suddenly, that irritation swelled into something darker. Sienna needed to be knocked down a peg or two.

She continued to watch with false interest as Sienna droned on and on, as if she would actually be interested in watching someone apply their own makeup. Was this what other girls really did for fun? Jasmin could think of way cooler things to do. Darker things.

"And finally, setting spray," Sienna concluded, spritzing her face with a fine mist. "It keeps everything in place."

When Sienna finally finished, she turned on her stool to face Jasmin directly. "How do I look?"

Jasmin faked a bright smile. "You look amazing!"

Sienna blushed, clearly pleased with the compliment. "Thanks." Then she gave Jasmin a shy smile that seemed oddly genuine. "Want me to do you?"

Jasmin sensed unexpected vulnerability in Sienna's facial expression and tone of voice. She really wanted to be friends. Too bad.

Jasmin grinned again. "First we have to do your hair. Do you have a headband?"

Sienna seemed confused for a second, then said, "I have a bow, but we have to tie it."

"That's fine," Jasmin said, fighting back her excitement. "Let your hair down, then give me the bow. I have just the style for you."

Sienna did as instructed, letting her long hair fall down her back. It was natural too, unlike Jasmin's own hair which only reached her shoulders. But that was neither here nor there.

Sienna handed her a silky red ribbon bow and turned back toward the mirror. Jasmin stood behind her, forcing a neutral expression. She pretended to contemplate how she was going to style Sienna's hair, then grabbed a handful as if she was going to put it in a ponytail.

"Up or down?" she asked, and Sienna blushed again.

"I think an updo would be cute."

Jasmin smirked and gathered Sienna's hair as if she was going to style it in an updo. Then suddenly, in one swift motion, she wrenched the bow around Sienna's neck, circling it tightly and squeezing.

Sienna's eyes popped open wide with shock. She jerked back in her chair, her fingers wildly grasping for the bow, trying desperately to loosen it to no avail. Jasmin's lips curved into that sinister smile once again as Sienna's eyes welled with tears and she frantically tried to get free.

"I could kill you right now, you know," Jasmin said in an even but menacing tone. "I could tell our parents it was an accident."

Sienna tried to cry out, but Jasmin squeezed tighter, constricting her airways further. Sienna's face reddened just like Jasmin had seen in the movie she'd watched one night when her mother thought she was asleep. How cool.

Sienna sputtered out a word that sounded like "please." Jasmin squeezed tighter, and Sienna's face started to turn purple. The girl's hands clawed desperately at the ribbon, but Jasmin had positioned it perfectly, making it nearly impossible to get leverage.

Jasmin leaned close to her ear and said, "If your mom and my dad end up together, I promise I'll slit both of your throats in your sleep."

Sienna gasped and continued to struggle to break free from the bow, tears streaming down her face, ruining the makeup she'd so carefully applied.

"They need to break up," Jasmin continued, her voice unnervingly calm. "Make that happen."

Sienna squeaked and nodded, and Jasmin immediately relented, loosening the bow. Sienna gasped for air now that she could breathe again, a wild and horrified look in her eyes. She coughed violently, one hand rubbing at her throat.

"I'm telling!" she finally mustered, her voice hoarse.

"Oh yeah?" Jasmin said sweetly. "And who are they gonna believe? You, the bully, or me, the victim? Time to wise up, Sienna. You're never gonna win this game."

Her eyes held a dark, calculating look as she moved around to face Sienna directly. "And besides, what I said earlier was a promise. You'll never see me coming."

Sienna and Jasmin stared at each other for a long time, a silent battle of wills. Sienna's eyes were wide with terror and disbelief, while Jasmin's remained cold and unblinking. Finally, Sienna visibly relented, her shoulders slumping in defeat.

Jasmin's lips curved into her infamous smile. "Good. Now clean up that neck. It's starting to bruise."

Sienna wordlessly turned back to her vanity mirror. Her hands trembled as she reached for concealer, dabbing it carefully along the angry red marks forming on her neck. Jasmin watched for a few seconds, then walked over to Sienna's bed and plopped down, making herself comfortable as if nothing unusual had happened.

"You know," Jasmin said conversationally as she leaned back against the pillows, "we could actually get along if you just accept how things are going to be."

Sienna didn't respond, focused on covering the evidence of what had just occurred. Her eyes in the mirror were haunted, her earlier confidence completely shattered.

"I mean, I'm not unreasonable," Jasmin continued, examining her fingernails. "If your mom breaks up with my dad, we can just go back to ignoring each other at school. No hard feelings."

Sienna's hand paused, the concealer brush hovering over her skin. "You're crazy," she whispered, her voice barely audible.

Jasmin smiled. "Maybe. But I'm also very, very patient."

For the next fifteen minutes, an oppressive silence filled the room. Sienna finished covering the marks on her neck and fixed her makeup, wiping away the tear tracks and reapplying her mascara. She kept shooting nervous glances at Jasmin, who remained sprawled comfortably on the bed, the picture of innocent relaxation.

When David's voice finally called out from the living room, "Girls! I brought ice cream!" Sienna flinched as if she'd been struck.

Jasmin sat up and smoothed her clothes. "Remember," she said quietly. "Our secret."

Sienna nodded, her eyes downcast.

"And cheer up," Jasmin added with mock concern. "They'll think something's wrong if you look so upset."

Then Jasmin opened the door and stepped into the hallway, her demeanor instantly transforming into that of an excited child. "Coming, Daddy!" she called, her voice bright and innocent.

Chapter 13

Jasmin led the way as Sienna followed slowly, her movements stiff and uncertain. As they walked down the hall toward the living room, Jasmin could practically feel the fear radiating from her former nemesis.

It was intoxicating.

In the living room, David and Shanika sat close together on the couch, bowls of ice cream in their hands. Two more bowls waited on the coffee table.

"There you are!" David said cheerfully. "We were starting to think you'd forgotten about dessert."

"Never," Jasmin said with a giggle, skipping over to claim her bowl.

Sienna moved more hesitantly, her smile tight as she took her own ice cream.

"So," Shanika asked, her tone warm and hopeful, "did you two have a good time getting to know each other?"

Jasmin beamed. "The best! Sienna showed me her makeup. She's really good at it."

All eyes turned to Sienna, who seemed to shrink under the attention. "Yeah," she managed. "It was... fun."

Shanika's brow furrowed, clearly sensing something was off with her daughter. "Are you feeling okay, honey? You look a little pale."

"I'm fine," Sienna said quickly. "Just a headache."

"Do you need some medicine?" Shanika asked, already half-rising from the couch.

"No!" Sienna's response came too forcefully. She took a breath and tried again. "No, thanks. It's not that bad."

David and Shanika exchanged concerned glances. Jasmin watched the interaction with interest, spooning ice cream into her mouth with exaggerated enjoyment.

"Well," David said after a moment, "I'm glad you girls are getting along. That means a lot to us."

Jasmin nodded enthusiastically. "Me too, Daddy. I think Sienna and I are going to be great friends."

She glanced at Sienna, who was staring down at her melting ice cream. "Right, Sienna?"

Sienna looked up, meeting Jasmin's gaze. For a second, something like defiance flickered in her eyes. Then it was gone, replaced by resignation.

"Right," she agreed quietly.

Jasmin smiled and took another bite of ice cream. This was going even better than she had hoped. With Sienna properly intimidated, the next phase of her plan could begin.

Christmas was getting closer but already she could feel victory within reach.

Her father would be home soon.

Her family would be whole.

And nothing and no one would stand in her way.

Chapter 14

The afternoon sun cast long shadows as David and Jasmin drove home from Shanika's apartment. Jasmin sat quietly in the passenger seat, staring out the window with a pensive expression. Inside, her mind was racing, analyzing the afternoon's events and planning her next move.

"You're awfully quiet over there," David observed, glancing at his daughter with a small smile. "Penny for your thoughts?"

Jasmin turned to look at him, her face arranged to appear thoughtful rather than calculating. "Just thinking about today."

"It seemed to go pretty well, don't you think? You and Sienna really hit it off."

Jasmin nodded slowly. "She's nice," she said, the lie coming easily. "She showed me her makeup."

"I noticed that," David chuckled. "Shanika's been teaching her. She's got a real talent for it."

Jasmin stayed quiet, watching her father's profile. He seemed relaxed, content. The visit had clearly gone the way he'd hoped it would.

"Daddy?" she asked, her voice suddenly small.

"Yes, princess?"

"Are you going to forget about me when you marry Shanika?"

David's hands tightened on the steering wheel, and he shot her a startled look. "What? No, of course not! Why would you even think that?"

Jasmin looked down at her hands, folded in her lap. "Because you'll have a new family. You'll have Sienna."

"Jasmin," David said firmly, "no one could ever replace you. You're my daughter, and I love you more than anything in the world."

"But you're going to live with them, right? And I'll just visit sometimes?"

David sighed, clearly uncomfortable with the direction of the conversation. "We haven't figured out all those details yet. But I promise you'll always be the most important person in my life."

Jasmin looked up at him, her eyes wide and vulnerable. "Then why would you choose Shanika? Mommy is just as beautiful as her, right?"

The car slowed as David's focus wavered. He cleared his throat. "Jasmin, that's... that's not what this is about. Your mother and I, well... it's complicated."

"What's complicated? Don't you love Mommy anymore?"

David's discomfort was now plainly visible. His shoulders tensed, and a frown line appeared between his eyebrows. "My decision was a grown-up decision, honey. Maybe you'll understand when you become an adult."

Jasmin stared at him, letting tears well up in her eyes. "You're still spending Christmas with me and Mommy though, right?"

The question clearly caught him off guard. He sputtered his response. "I... well, I was thinking maybe you could spend the morning with your mother and then you, Sienna, Shanika and I could—"

She didn't let him finish the sentence before belting out a cry of dismay.

"How could you?" she screeched, her voice filling the small space of the car. "We always spend Christmas together as a family. How could you?"

Tears streamed down her cheeks, and the emotion wasn't entirely feigned. The thought of spending Christmas with Shanika and Sienna instead of her mother was genuinely upsetting. Christmas had always been special—the three of them in matching pajamas, opening presents together by the tree, her mother's special breakfast, her father reading "'Twas the Night Before Christmas" on Christmas Eve. The idea of losing that tradition hurt more than she expected.

David looked distraught at her outburst. He reached over to touch her arm, but she jerked away. "Listen, baby girl," he said, his voice gentle. "It's going to be okay. We're all going to get through this together."

"How can we," she cried, "when you and that woman are ruining everything!"

They had just pulled into the driveway of her mother's house. Before David could respond, Jasmin unclipped her seatbelt and flung open the car door, not even waiting for her father to put the car in park. She thundered toward the front door, which her mother was just opening, likely having heard them arrive.

"Jasmin, what's—" Malia began, but Jasmin roughly pushed past her and ran straight to her bedroom, slamming the door behind her.

Through the door, Jasmin heard her mother's confused voice. "What the hell—"

Jasmin pressed her ear against the wood, listening intently. She had to play this just right to get them to have an extended conversation. Her whole body tensed with anticipation.

"What happened?" Malia's voice came through, concern evident in her tone.

"She's just really upset," David tried to explain, his voice weary.

"Well, what did you expect, David?" Malia's voice rose . "You can't just force a whole other family down her throat, especially this close to Christmas!"

Jasmin's lips curved into a satisfied smile. Her mother was playing right into her hands without even realizing it.

David spoke his next words in a hushed tone, but Jasmin strained her ears to catch every word.

"She wants us to spend Christmas together."

Silence fell for a second before Malia replied, "Well, is that what you want?"

More silence followed, and Jasmin almost wanted to creep out of her bedroom into the hallway to hear them better, but she couldn't risk blowing her cover.

Finally, David spoke again. "You know I never wanted us to get divorced, but everything just became too much, Malia."

Jasmin's ears perked up. This was going better than expected. She pressed her ear harder against the door.

"I don't want a divorce either, but you're the one who left us," her mother said, her voice softer now, vulnerable.

More silence stretched between them. Jasmin held her breath, her heart pounding in her chest.

Then David finally spoke again. "Look, I'll have to talk to Shanika because she was looking forward to us spending Christmas together. We were thinking it would be a way for the girls to bond, and—"

"So you're really standing here telling me that?" Malia cut in, her voice hardening again. "I don't give a damn about that broad or her daughter!"

"Look, I'm not here to argue with you, okay?" David's tone turned angry. "I'll leave now. We'll talk about Christmas later."

"Yeah, you do that," Malia said sarcastically.

The front door slammed, and Jasmin hurried to her window, peering through the curtains to see her father striding back to his car, his movements stiff with frustration. She watched as he backed out of the driveway and drove away, his tires squealing on the pavement.

A pool of hope fluttered in Jasmin's belly. Maybe her parents weren't done with each other after all. Her father had admitted he never wanted the divorce. Her mother had said the same. All they needed was a little push to remember what they once had.

Chapter 15

The aroma of Malia's home-cooked meal filled the dining room as Jasmin took another bite of her perfectly seasoned chicken. Her mother had outdone herself tonight—the chicken was juicy, the rice fluffy, and the vegetables crisp-tender. It was exactly the way Jasmin liked it.

Things seemed to be turning around. After the drama of the afternoon, the evening had settled into something almost normal. Almost like before, when her father still lived with them and they ate dinner together every night.

"This is really good, Mom," Jasmin said, offering a genuine smile.

"Thank you, sweetie," Malia replied, her own smile warm but tinged with something Jasmin couldn't quite identify. Concern, maybe. Or curiosity.

After a few moments of companionable silence, Malia gently cleared her throat. "So you were really upset earlier when you came back from Sienna's house. Did something happen while you were there?"

Jasmin looked up at the way her mother said it. There was that knowing look again. How did her mother always seem to know? Jasmin had read online about mother's intuition, but it was freaky to see it play out in real life.

"No, nothing happened," she lied effortlessly. "I just don't like them. Daddy keeps trying to bring us together, but our family got along just fine. He doesn't belong with them. He belongs with us."

Malia sat in silence as if contemplating how to respond to her daughter. Jasmin watched her mother's face, trying to read her thoughts. Was she angry? Sad? Hopeful?

Then Malia finally spoke, a softness in her tone and eyes. "Jasmin, I understand you don't want me and your father to get a divorce, but—"

"You two don't want it either!" Jasmin belted, then almost clapped a hand over her mouth. She hadn't meant to say that aloud. She quickly recovered. "I see how you two still love each other. Why can't we just be a family again?"

Malia sat silently for a long time, her fork pushing rice around her plate. When she finally looked up, her eyes were filled with tears. "It's going to be okay, honey. Right now things are tough, but they will all work out in the end."

Jasmin didn't bother to respond to that because she didn't want to argue with her mother. Besides, what was there to say? Adults always said things would work out, but they rarely specified how. Jasmin knew what she had to do. If her parents wouldn't fix this themselves, she would have to do it for them.

After dinner, Jasmin helped clear the table, then prepared for bed. She brushed her teeth, put on her pajamas, and even read a book for a while—all the things she normally did before sleep. But sleep was the furthest thing from her mind tonight.

When she was sure her mother was safely in her own bedroom with the door closed, Jasmin retrieved her secret phone from its hiding place. The screen lit up her face in the dimness of her room as she quickly logged into the game.

Her heart leaped when she saw that SnakeEyes77 was already online. She couldn't wait to report the day's developments to him. They barely played for two minutes before she told him what was going on and how she needed to get rid of Shanika and her daughter immediately.

Calm down, he replied. **We'll figure this out together. I have a plan.**

What could we possibly do? she asked, her fingers flying across the screen.

I have an idea, but you need to hack into Shanika's phone for it to work.

Jasmin was puzzled. **How am I supposed to do that? I don't even have her phone number.**

He took a few moments before responding. **Is she on social media?**

Jasmin quickly typed back, **Yes.**

Okay, then that will work. Here's what you do.

Jasmin's eyes pored over every word of his instruction. She didn't know if she could pull it off, but she read intently as SnakeEyes77 laid out his plan. It was devious, more complex than anything she'd tried before, but also brilliant in its simplicity.

She opened a web browser and searched for Shanika on social media. Within minutes, she had found her profile—it was connected to her father's since they had named each other in their relationship statuses, which made things much easier. She searched through Shanika's photos and posts, looking for what SnakeEyes77 had told her to find.

Her eyes lit up when she found it. **Got him!** she quickly reported.

In a photo from three years ago, she had spotted him—a man with his arm around Shanika, with a younger Sienna standing in front of them. The caption read: **Co-parenting isn't always easy, but we make it work for our princess. Happy birthday, Sienna! Love, Mom and Dad.**

Good, SnakeEyes77 responded. **Now create the profile. Make sure you get all the details right. It has to work.**

She did as he instructed, working intently to create a replica of the profile of Shanika's ex-boyfriend, who also happened to be Sienna's father. She used the photos she could find from Shanika's timeline, plus a few more she found when she discovered his real profile. She filled in details about his hometown, his job, his interests—all information gleaned from what little was publicly visible.

Done, she said after thirty minutes of careful work.

Good. Now send her a friend request. Tell her your other profile was hacked. If she bites the bait, we're in.

Jasmin did as he said, crafting a simple message to accompany the friend request: **Hey Shanika, my account got hacked last week. Had to create a new profile. This is Devaughn.**

She sent it and waited with bated breath. Five minutes later, the friend request was accepted.

She accepted, Jasmin said with a smile.

SnakeEyes77 sent hand clap emojis. **Good. We're in.**

Jasmin's heart raced as she began implementing their plan. It was risky, but if it worked, it could solve all her problems.

She sent a casual message to Shanika as Devaughn: **Been thinking about you and Sienna a lot lately. How are you two doing?**

While she waited for a response, Jasmin's mind whirled with possibilities. If Shanika thought her ex was interested in getting back together, would she reconsider her relationship with David? And if David saw Shanika pulling away, would he realize that he belonged with Malia?

A response from Shanika appeared: **We're good. Sienna's getting so big. Middle school next year, can you believe it?**

Jasmin smiled to herself. This was going to be easier than she thought.

I know, our little girl is growing up fast, she wrote back. **I've been doing a lot of thinking lately about us, about the mistakes I made. I miss what we had.**

She stared at the screen, her pulse quickening as she saw the typing indicator appear and disappear several times. Shanika was clearly thinking hard about her response.

Finally: **Devaughn, we've been over this. We're better as co-parents than we ever were as a couple.**

I know, Jasmin typed, trying to capture what she imagined would be the voice of a regretful ex. **But people change. I've changed. Just been thinking a lot about**

family lately, especially with Christmas coming up. Sienna deserves to have both her parents together.

Another long pause before Shanika replied: **I'm seeing someone, Davaughn. It's serious.**

Jasmin smiled to herself. This was exactly what she wanted—a chance to plant seeds of doubt about her father.

That David guy? she typed. **Sienna mentioned him. Seems like he's already got a family of his own.**

Three dots appeared, disappeared, then appeared again as Shanika composed her response. **It's complicated, but we're working it out. His daughter and Sienna are getting along.**

That's not what Sienna told me, Jasmin wrote, her heart racing at her own boldness. **She said the other girl is a brat and the guy mentioned to her that he's still hung up on his soon to be ex wife.**

The response took even longer this time: **When did you talk to Sienna about this?**

Jasmin realized she'd made a tactical error. She quickly backtracked: **She called me last week, just catching up. Probably shouldn't have said anything. You know how kids exaggerate.**

I didn't know you two were in touch, came the response.

Just occasionally, Jasmin wrote. **Father-daughter stuff. Listen, there's this family trip coming up for my job in January. We are supposed to go to the aquarium. You know how Sienna loves animals. Here's the link. Check it out and let me know what you think.**

The typing indicator appeared, disappeared, and finally, Shanika responded: **I'll think about it and check with Sienna. No promises.**

That's all I'm asking, Jasmin replied. **Night, Shanika.**

She closed the messaging app and reported back to SnakeEyes77: **Phase one complete. I sent her the link. Let me know if she opens it.**

Five minutes later, SnakeEyes77 wrote back. **We're in.**

Jasmin's eyes were tired but her heart leapt with excitement. **What's next?**

I'll take it from here, he said. **The rest of this is for adult eyes only. Merry Christmas little tyke.**

Jasmin giggled with glee. **What are you going to do?**

She half-expected for SnakeEyes77 to tell her that the rest of the plan was "Grown Folks Business" but he didn't. Instead, he said, **Let's just say that Sienna's mother and father are about to be reunited from a dating app. Now that I have access to her phone, it will look like all the messages are coming from her to her ex. Shanika and Sienna will be off your hands in no time.**

Jasmin blinked back happy tears. **How will I know the plan worked?**

SnakeEyes77 responded immediately. **I'll let you know when the time is right. I'll need you for the final part of the plan.**

Jasmin gasped and her heart filled with glee. He actually thought she was smart enough to help him pull this off?

Okay, I'll be on standby, she wrote back.

Jasmin put the phone away, blinking back happy tears as a feeling of satisfaction spread through her. For the first time since her father had announced he was leaving, she felt truly in control of the situation. She was no longer just a powerless kid being dragged along by the decisions of adults. She was taking action, steering her family back to where it belonged.

As she drifted off to sleep that night, she imagined Christmas morning—her family together again, her parents smiling at each other across the breakfast table, Shanika and Sienna nowhere in sight. It was a beautiful vision, and she was determined to make it reality.

***

Sunday flew by in a blur of homework, texting, and careful monitoring of the fake social media account, but Monday morning arrived with a surprise. When Jasmin came down for breakfast, she found her mother already at the kitchen table, dressed in a crisp blue blouse and tailored black pants, her laptop open in front of her and a coffee mug steaming at her elbow.

"Why are you all dressed up?" Jasmin asked, taking in her mother's polished appearance.

Malia took a deep breath, a smile spreading across her face. "I start my new job today."

Jasmin stared at her mother for a while, processing this unexpected information. "Congratulations," she finally said.

"Thank you," Malia replied, her eyes bright with a confidence Jasmin hadn't seen in a long time.

Jasmin grabbed a banana and her backpack, her mind racing. Her mother had a job? When had that happened? And what did it mean for their family, for her plans?

As she headed to school, Jasmin pondered this new development. On one hand, her mother getting a job was a good thing—it meant she was moving forward, becoming stronger and more independent. But on the other hand, would this make it harder to bring her parents back together? If her mother was building a new life without her father, would she even want him back?

Jasmin shook her head, pushing away the doubt. No, this didn't change anything. Her mother still loved her father—she'd seen it in her eyes when they'd talked about the divorce. And her father still loved her mother; he'd admitted as much.

All she needed to do was remove the obstacles in their path. Shanika was the final domino that needed to fall. Once she was out of the picture, everything else would fall into place.

Chapter 16

The days following her first social media interaction with Shanika passed in a blur for Jasmin. Each day at school, she kept a watchful eye on Sienna, noting with satisfaction that the other girl seemed to be keeping her distance. She sat in front of Jasmin during first period and never turned around. Whenever they passed in the hallway, Sienna would duck her head and hurry in the opposite direction. In the art class they shared, Sienna chose a seat as far from Jasmin as possible.

It was all very satisfying. Sienna was remaining "in line," exactly as Jasmin wanted. What she had said during their conversation at Shanika's apartment had clearly hit its mark. One obstacle was effectively neutralized.

But as the week progressed, Jasmin grew increasingly anxious about the other part of her plan. SnakeEyes77 hadn't sent any messages since their last conversation on Sunday night. Christmas was barely a week away now. Why hadn't he given any updates? Had something gone wrong? Had he abandoned the plan—abandoned her?

Each night, Jasmin would retrieve her secret phone from its hiding place, log into the game, and check for messages. Each night, she was met with disappointment. No word from SnakeEyes77.

By Thursday, doubt had begun to creep in. Maybe this plan was too elaborate, too risky. Maybe it wouldn't work after all. Maybe she should try something else, something simpler.

Then finally, on Thursday evening, the message came through on the gaming app. Jasmin's heart leaped when she saw SnakeEyes77's username appear on her screen.

When's the next time you are supposed to go over Shanika's house? he asked, without any greeting or explanation for his absence.

Jasmin quickly replied, her fingers trembling with excitement. **Saturday.**

He wrote back seconds later: **Good. The final part of the plan is ready. But you have to play your part well.**

Jasmin was eager to please him. **I will. Just tell me what to do.**

Once again, he sent her instructions, and once again, her lips curved into a smile as she read them. This wouldn't be easy, but she would make it happen. The plan was more daring than anything she'd attempted before, but if it worked, it would solve all her problems in one swoop.

She spent the next hour going over the details with SnakeEyes77, asking questions and memorizing her role. By the time she put the phone away, she felt both nervous and exhilarated. Saturday couldn't come fast enough.

***

When Jasmin got home from school on Friday, her mother was sitting on the couch dressed in regular clothes.

She greeted Jasmin with a smile. "Hey, sweetie. How was school?"

"Fine," Jasmin replied automatically, her eyes narrowing. Something was different. Her mother was practically glowing, a far cry from the tired, sad woman who had been shuffling around the house just a couple of weeks ago. "What's up?"

Malia's smile widened. "I have some exciting news for you. Your father and I agreed to spend Christmas morning together with you as a family."

Jasmin almost dropped her backpack in shock. Her parents had agreed to spend Christmas together? Without her having to manipulate them into it? Pure joy swelled within her. It was happening! Her family was coming back together!

But her mother continued, a careful look on her face. "But I want to tell you this, Jasmin: This doesn't mean we're getting back together. We just want to find a healthy way to navigate the holidays as a family. Your dad wants to bring you to Shanika and Sienna's house for Christmas afternoon."

Jasmin barely listened to the rest of her mother's words. If Daddy was coming home Christmas morning, he wasn't leaving. She would make sure of it. By Christmas afternoon, Shanika would be out of the picture entirely, if her plan with SnakeEyes77 worked.

"So what do you think?" Malia asked, bringing Jasmin's attention back to the present. "Are you okay with that arrangement?"

Jasmin forced herself to look thoughtful, as if considering the proposal, when inside she was doing cartwheels of joy. "Yeah, I think that sounds good," she said, trying to keep her voice neutral. "Will Daddy stay for breakfast?"

"Yes, we thought we'd do presents and then have breakfast together, just like we used to," Malia said, her voice modulated to sound casual, though Jasmin caught the flicker of emotion in her eyes.

"That's perfect," Jasmin said, unable to keep the smile from her face. "It'll be just like old times."

Malia's expression softened. "For the morning, yes. But remember, honey, your dad will be taking you to Shanika's afterward. We've agreed that you'll spend the afternoon with them, and then your dad will bring you back here for dinner."

Jasmin nodded, though inwardly she was thinking that none of that would be necessary once her plan was executed.

Chapter 17

Jasmin was about to ask her mother if she could get a snack from the kitchen when they heard a knock on the front door. Jasmin turned back to face it, then stared at her mother, who now wore a beaming smile on her face.

"Go ahead and answer it," Malia said, gesturing.

Jasmin wasn't sure how to respond, but she obeyed her mother, moving forward to pull open the door.

David was standing there with a huge smile on his face.

Jasmin's heart fluttered. "Daddy?"

His smile widened. "That's right, I'm here, baby girl. Did your mother tell you what we're about to do?"

Jasmin was caught off guard. She glanced back at Malia, who was still smiling, before turning to her father again. "No... what is it?"

David beamed. "We're going Christmas tree shopping, just like old times."

Jasmin's heart leaped. Her plan was working better than she thought. "Yes!" she shouted, barely able to contain her excitement. She hadn't expected her parents to fall back into old traditions so quickly, but this was perfect. Tree shopping had always been a family affair, with the three of them wandering through rows of evergreens, arguing good-naturedly over which one was the perfect height, fullness, and shape.

"I'll be right back!" she exclaimed, hurriedly rushing to ditch her backpack in her room. As she threw it on her bed, her mind raced with possibilities. Maybe she wouldn't need the final phase of SnakeEyes77's plan after all. Maybe her parents were already finding their way back to each other naturally.

She rushed back to the living room, eager to leave with her father, but then noticed Malia grabbing her coat too.

"Where are you going?" Jasmin asked, unable to keep the suspicion from her voice.

Malia looked at Jasmin, then David. "I thought it would be nice if we all went together."

The atmosphere immediately shifted. The easy smile on David's face faded, replaced by a tense, guarded expression. "I'm not sure that's a good idea, Malia."

Malia cocked her head to the side, her own smile turning brittle. "And why not?"

David started, then stopped, then started again. "I don't want anyone getting the wrong idea."

"Wrong idea about what?" she pressed. "We're spending Christmas as a family. Why not go tree shopping as a family too?"

David swallowed, his discomfort palpable. "Come on. Don't make this a fight."

"It doesn't have to be a fight if we agree to be cordial."

"Come on, Malia. You know that's not fair. I have a girlfriend, remember?"

"You also have a wife."

The tension thickened, filling the room like a heavy fog. Jasmin stood frozen between her parents, watching as the pleasant afternoon she had anticipated crumbled before her eyes.

David chuckled roughly, a harsh sound devoid of humor. "Oh so you're really doing this? In front of our daughter?"

Malia scoffed. "You have no problem doing everything else in front of her."

"What the hell is that supposed to mean? And I know you ain't talking, when it's your disloyalty toward our daughter that got us in this situation in the first place!"

Jasmin cringed, not expecting her father to have mentioned that. She knew exactly what he was referring to. Their former next-door neighbor, old Miss Bertha, was once one of Jasmin's enemies. Things started small between them until they culminated in the disappearance of Miss Bertha's beloved cat, Scruffles.

Miss Bertha swore it was Jasmin who had something to do with it, and Malia believed it too, but David didn't. Nothing could be proven. Miss Bertha sold her house and moved away shortly thereafter, but Jasmin never would have thought that her actions played a role in her parent's split.

Malia took a step back in shock at David's words. "My disloyalty?" she said, her voice rising with indignation. "Says the man who leaves our house one day and pops up with a new girlfriend a month later!"

"Don't make this about me, Malia! You're the fucking liar!"

"Don't you fucking cuss at me in front of my daughter!"

Both of them were heaving with anger, faces flushed, bodies rigid with tension. Jasmin's eyes went back and forth between them like a ping pong match, her earlier excitement replaced by a sinking feeling in her stomach. This wasn't how it was supposed to go.

David spoke again in a softer but threatening tone. "Let's not do this, okay? I just want a nice Christmas for my baby girl."

Malia didn't stand down. "She's our baby girl, or did you forget that since you're so busy sniffing around Shanika and her daughter?"

David scoffed. "You're impossible."

"I just call it how I see it, honey."

David seemed to have had enough. His face darkened, and when he spoke again, his voice was low and dangerous. "You over there acting all high and mighty about me finding someone else, but did you think about how you destroyed our family with what you did at your job? You're lucky you're not in prison!"

"I told you, that wasn't me," Malia said in a deadly tone, but David was past this argument.

"Whatever Malia. One of these days you are going to have to face the consequences for your actions. That's what you need to be teaching our daughter: integrity. Not embezzling funds from a company for five years."

Malia gasped as if she couldn't believe he went there. Her hand moved before Jasmin could process what was happening, connecting with David's cheek in a sharp slap. "You bastard!"

She looked at Jasmin as if trying to assess the damage that David's revelation might have caused. But Jasmin already knew about the situation. She had heard her parents argue about it several times while they thought she was sleeping—hushed, heated discussions about missing money, an internal investigation, Malia's insistence that she was being framed, David's growing doubt.

"Look, I'm not trying to fight with you today, Malia," David said in a tired tone, rubbing his cheek. "I just wanna take my daughter tree shopping. Can we do that?"

Malia stared for a long time before her eyes welled with tears. "Go ahead. Go on without me!" She hurried to her room and slammed the door.

David stared after her for a while before he finally turned to Jasmin. "Ready to go?" he asked, his voice strained, the cheerfulness of his earlier greeting completely gone.

Jasmin nodded but her hope had already deflated. If her parents were arguing like this, was there even a chance of them getting back together? The viciousness of their exchange had shaken her. She had known they were having problems, of course—that's why her father had left in the first place—but seeing them tear into each other like that made her wonder if some wounds were too deep to heal.

"Let's go, then," David said, holding the door open for her.

Chapter 18

Saturday morning dawned bright and clear, a perfect December day. Jasmin woke early, her stomach fluttering with nervous anticipation. Today was the day. The culmination of all her planning and scheming.

She held a bit of hope in her chest since she heard her mother and father apologizing to each other over the phone last night after her father dropped her off, but that wasn't enough. Today had to be the final nail in the coffin for David and Shanika's relationship if Jasmin's parents had any chance of getting back together.

She checked her secret phone first thing, relieved to find a message from SnakeEyes77: **Everything's set for today. Remember, timing is crucial. Text me when you're in position.**

I will, she replied simply.

She dressed carefully, choosing an outfit that made her look innocent—a pastel sweater, jeans, and sneakers. She styled her hair in two braids with bobos, which she normally wouldn't be caught dead wearing, but today was about playing a role.

"You look nice," Malia commented when Jasmin came down for breakfast. "Excited to see your dad?"

Jasmin nodded, unable to keep a smile from her face. "Yeah. What time is he picking me up?"

"Eleven," Malia replied, sliding a plate of pancakes in front of her. "He said Shanika's making lunch for y'all."

Jasmin nodded again, keeping her expression neutral. "Cool."

At precisely eleven o'clock, the doorbell rang. Jasmin's heart skipped a beat as her mother went to answer it. She heard her father's voice in the hallway, exchanging pleasantries with Malia. There was a warmth to their interaction that hadn't been there before, a hint of the easy rapport they'd once shared.

Jasmin took a deep breath, steeling herself. Today would determine whether that warmth became a permanent fixture once again.

"Hey, princess," David said as he entered the kitchen, his smile wide and genuine. "Ready to go?"

Jasmin nodded, grabbing her jacket from the back of her chair. "Ready."

When David texted to invite Jasmin over to Shanika's apartment for Saturday evening, she'd assumed it would be another "family bonding" attempt with Sienna.

But when she arrived at Shanika's apartment, something felt off.

"Where's Sienna?" Jasmin asked as they entered and didn't see Sienna standing next to her mother, who was waiting at the front door.

David hesitated before answering. "She's not here today."

Before Jasmin could press for more information, Shanika cut in. "Hi, Jasmin," she greeted with a smile that seemed just a touch too bright. "Come on in. Make yourself comfortable."

Jasmin glanced around the apartment.

"Where's Sienna?" she asked again, this time directing the question at Shanika.

Shanika exchanged a quick look with David before her smile widened. "Sienna is away with her grandmother. My sister takes care of our mother, and Sienna went there to spend time before the holiday."

Jasmin frowned, confused by this unexpected development. "So why am I here then?"

An awkward silence fell over the room. Shanika's smile faltered, and she glanced at David as if seeking backup.

David cleared his throat. "We thought it would be nice for you and Shanika to get to know each other a little more."

Jasmin's mind filled with alarm. "Me and Shanika? Are you leaving too?" The last thing she wanted was to be left alone with this woman who was trying to take her father away from her family.

But David shook his head with a chuckle. "Of course not, baby girl. We're all gonna spend a few hours together, maybe watch a movie or something. You like movies, right?"

Jasmin almost sighed in exasperation. Why was her father trying to force this relationship? It was one thing to try to make her and Sienna get along, but what was she supposed to talk about with a grown woman who was dating her father?

Still, she smiled and said, "Sure!"

"Great," David said, visibly relieved.

The trio awkwardly shifted to the living room, where Jasmin slumped onto the couch between David and Shanika.

David casually picked up the remote and searched for a movie.

Jasmin froze when she saw "It's a Wonderful Life" prominently featured in the "Suggested for You" section.

That was their movie—hers, her mother's, and her father's. They had watched it every Christmas season for as long as Jasmin could remember, usually while decorating the tree or wrapping presents. It was tradition, sacred and inviolable.

"What about this one?" he asked, nervousness etching his features.

Jasmin fought the urge to glower at him. "Sure," she forced out.

David selected the movie, and they settled in to watch. As the familiar opening credits began to roll, Jasmin felt a wave of homesickness wash over her. This was all wrong. She should be watching this with her mother, in their apartment, with their tree.

They were about ten minutes into the film when David suddenly paused it. "You know what we're missing?" he said, glancing between Jasmin and Shanika. "Gourmet popcorn!"

Jasmin's jaw clenched. That was the snack they always shared as a family—fancy popcorn from the specialty shop near their house, with different flavors like caramel, cheddar cheese, and white chocolate. Daddy was doing way too much to impress this woman and trying too hard to make Jasmin like her.

David shot a quick look at Shanika, then Jasmin. "How about I go to the store and grab some? You two can chat while I'm gone."

Jasmin opened her mouth to say, "Hell no," but Shanika said, "Sure, that would be great!" before she could get the words out.

Then Jasmin thought about it. If David was gone, that would make the next part of her plan easier. She'd been messaging with SnakeEyes77 all week about the "final phase," and he'd instructed her to be ready for an opportunity just like this.

"Yeah, sure," Jasmin agreed, trying to sound casual. "Go ahead."

David beamed, clearly pleased by her seeming enthusiasm. "I'll be back in about thirty minutes. You two behave yourselves," he added with a wink that made Jasmin want to roll her eyes.

After David left, Shanika turned to Jasmin with a warm smile that didn't quite reach her eyes. "So, how's school going? David mentioned you made honor roll?"

Jasmin nodded, pretending to be interested while staring at the paused movie on the TV screen. "Yeah, I did. I'm ready for middle school next year."

"That's great. I remember when I was in school," Shanika offered. "I loved it."

"Cool," Jasmin replied flatly.

Shanika tried again. "Your dad also mentioned you're quite the gamer? Sienna loves video games too."

"Mostly just one game," Jasmin corrected her. "Royal Realm. It's an MMORPG."

"Oh, I'm not familiar with that one," Shanika said. "But I've heard of World of Warcraft. Is it similar?"

"Not really," Jasmin said, suppressing a sigh. She didn't expect Shanika to understand gaming, and she certainly didn't want to have a bonding moment over it.

After a few more attempts at small talk that Jasmin shut down with monosyllabic responses, an awkward silence fell between them. Shanika fidgeted with her soda can, clearly uncomfortable.

"Would you like something else to drink?" she finally asked. "Water, maybe, or hot chocolate?"

"Actually, could I use your bathroom?" Jasmin asked.

Shanika seemed relieved at the reprieve. "Of course. Down the hall, second door on the left."

Jasmin hurried to the bathroom, locking the door behind her. She pulled out her secret phone from the inner pocket of her jacket, heart racing as she opened the gaming app to message SnakeEyes77. He was supposed to be on standby for their plan, and she hoped he would follow through.

To her relief, he was online, just as he had promised.

Dad went to the store. It's just me and Shanika.

Good. Keep your phone on and with you. I'll set things up on my end and you do your part.

Jasmin grew nervous. This was the moment of truth. **What if I'm not able to do what we discussed?**

A few moments passed before SnakeEyes77 wrote back. **You'll make a way. I have faith in you.**

That gave her the encouragement she needed.

Okay. I got this.

A few more moments, and then: **Indeed you do.**

Jasmin tucked the phone back into her pocket and flushed the toilet for show. She washed her hands, taking a moment to compose her expression as she stared at herself in the mirror.

When she emerged from the bathroom, Shanika was standing right outside the door, which startled Jasmin momentarily. The woman was giving her a strange, assessing look.

"What were you doing in there?" Shanika asked, her tone suspicious.

Jasmin feigned innocence, her heart pounding. "Using the bathroom?"

Shanika stared at her for a long moment, as if trying to read her thoughts. Had she heard Jasmin texting SnakeEyes77? Or noticed the glow of the phone screen under the door?

Finally, Shanika's expression softened, and she shook her head. "Sorry, I just... You were in there for a while."

"Oh," Jasmin said with a small laugh. "I was doing a number two."

Shanika made a stank face, though she didn't look entirely convinced. "Let's go back to the living room. Your dad should be back soon."

Chapter 19

As they returned to the couch, Jasmin considered her approach. She needed to play this carefully for the plan to work.

"So," Shanika said after a moment, clearly trying to restart their stilted conversation, "are you excited about Christmas?"

Jasmin shrugged, allowing a hint of her genuine sadness to show. "I guess. It's different this year."

"I'm sure it is," Shanika said softly. "Adjustments can be hard."

"Yeah," Jasmin agreed, seeing her opening. "Especially with everything else going on."

Shanika tilted her head, curious. "What do you mean?"

Jasmin hesitated, as if uncertain whether to continue. "It's just... my mom's been having a rough time. Not just because of the divorce, but... other stuff."

"I'm sorry to hear that," Shanika said, sounding genuinely concerned. "Is there anything I can do?"

Jasmin shook her head, looking down at her hands. "I don't think so." She remained expressionless for a few moments, then purposefully brightened her demeanor. "Hey, do you have an extra blanket I can use? It's a little chilly in here."

Shanika looked confused. "Chilly? You're cold?"

Jasmin nodded and forced a nervous smile.

Shanika stood, setting her phone on the end table. "I'll grab that for you."

Jasmin rose as well, trailing a few steps behind as Shanika moved toward the hallway. Catching the movement, Shanika glanced back with mild surprise but didn't say anything. They continued down the hall to the closet. Shanika turned the knob and pulled it open, revealing shelves of neatly folded linens.

"Let's see..." Shanika reached up toward the top shelf where several blankets were stacked. She stepped inside to get better leverage. "I think the blue one would be nice. Or there's a beige one if you prefer something warmer."

Jasmin didn't respond. As Shanika stretched upward, her back to the door, Jasmin seized her moment. With a quick, forceful shove, she pushed Shanika fully into the closet, causing her to stumble forward against the shelves.

"What—" Shanika began, but Jasmin had already slammed the door shut.

Moving quickly, Jasmin dragged a decorative chair from the hallway and wedged it firmly under the doorknob. The handle rattled immediately.

"Jasmin? What are you doing?" Shanika's voice came muffled through the door, confusion quickly giving way to alarm. "This isn't funny. Open the door right now!"

Jasmin backed away, breathing heavily, her heart pounding in her chest. She stood frozen, listening to Shanika's increasingly desperate calls.

"Jasmin! Let me out!" The door shook as Shanika pushed against it from inside, but the chair held firm. "Why are you doing this? Your father will be back any minute!"

"That's exactly what I'm counting on," Jasmin muttered, turning away from the closet and hurrying back to the living room. Behind her, Shanika's pleas grew more insistent, punctuated by the sound of fists hammering against wood.

With Shanika trapped, Jasmin hurried back to the living room and snatched the phone from the end table. Her fingers flew across the screen, navigating to the app SnakeEyes77 had told her about. The icon was discreet—something most people would overlook unless they knew what to look for.

"Perfect," she whispered, quickly moving the app to Shanika's main home screen where it couldn't be missed. She opened it and found exactly what she needed—conversations between Shanika and Devaughn, Sienna's father.

The messages made her stomach turn. Suggestive texts and photos from the past week, all exchanged right under her father's nose. Some of the pictures looked like they'd been pulled from Shanika's regular photo gallery—innocent images repurposed to seem flirtatious in this new context.

From the closet, Jasmin heard gasping, then rapid, shallow breathing. Shanika's voice came between desperate gulps of air. "Jasmin! Please! I can't—I can't breathe in here!"

The panicked edge in Shanika's voice gave Jasmin pause. Poor woman. She actually was claustrophobic. For a fleeting moment, guilt crept in, but she pushed it away. This was necessary. Her father would be back any minute.

Jasmin returned the chair to its original position and yanked the closet door open before dashing toward the apartment's entrance. She unlocked and cracked open the front door—an escape route if needed.

Behind her, the closet remained quiet. Then came shuffling sounds as Shanika slowly emerged. Her braids were disheveled, mascara streaking down her tear-stained cheeks. She braced herself against the wall, still struggling to regulate her breathing.

"Why would you do that, you little bitch?" Shanika's voice cracked with emotion, her usual composure shattered.

The front door swung open wider as David stepped in, clutching a bag of gourmet popcorn. His expression shifted from cheerful to confused as he took in the scene—Shanika's distress, Jasmin's wide-eyed look, the tension hanging palpable in the air.

"What the hell is going on?" he demanded, gaze darting between them.

Shanika opened her mouth, but Jasmin seized her moment.

"She's cheating on you!" she blurted, her voice carrying the perfect blend of shock and indignation. "I saw it on her phone!"

"What?" Shanika lunged forward, reaching for her device in Jasmin's hand.

Jasmin scurried behind her father. "Daddy, don't let her hurt me!" she cried, clutching his arm. "She got mad because I saw the messages. She tried to grab it from me—

that's why I ran for the door! I was about to leave when you came in!"

David's face hardened as he placed a protective arm around Jasmin. "Shanika, what's—"

"David, I swear I don't know what she's talking about," Shanika interrupted, her voice trembling. "Your daughter locked me in my closet! She—"

The sound of footsteps on the doorstep silenced her. A tall figure appeared in the doorway—Devaughn, Sienna's father, his broad shoulders filling the frame. He stepped inside like he belonged there.

"It's him!" Jasmin pointed dramatically. "That's who she's cheating with!"

The color drained from David's face as he locked eyes with Devaughn. The two men squared off, tension crackling between them.

"What the fuck are you doing here?" David's voice was dangerously low.

Devaughn's expression darkened. "I'm here to see my woman. What the hell are you doing here?"

Shanika stood frozen, her gaze bouncing between the two men. "Devaughn, what the hell are you talking about?"

A slow, knowing smile spread across Devaughn's face. "Don't act brand new now, baby. What was all that shit you was talking on the phone? You miss daddy, don't you?" His eyes suddenly registered Jasmin's presence. "Oh, my fault, baby girl."

Jasmin seized the moment of confusion to thrust the phone into her father's hands, the incriminating messages displayed on screen. "Look, Dad."

David's jaw tightened as he scrolled through the exchanges, his expression hardening with each flick of his thumb. After a long, painful silence, he looked up at Shanika.

"Oh, so this is how you feel?" The quiet hurt in his voice was worse than any shouting.

Shanika stepped forward, desperation in her eyes. "David, whatever she's showing you is not true! I don't know what's going on. Your daughter just locked me in my own closet!"

Jasmin gasped dramatically. "Daddy, she's lying about me!"

Devaughn surveyed the scene with growing impatience. "Look, bro," he said, cutting through the tension. "I don't know what's going on here, but I think you and your daughter need to leave. You had your time with Shanika, but it's time for me and my woman to get back together."

Jasmin held her breath, worried the men might come to blows. But David merely shook his head, a cold resignation settling over his features. He handed the phone to Devaughn, his movements deliberate and final.

"You got that, bro. I'm done here." He turned to Jasmin. "Let's go."

As David guided her out, Jasmin stole one last glance over her shoulder. Shanika stood frozen in disbelief, her world collapsing around her. Devaughn looked equally confused, holding the phone like he wasn't sure what to do with it.

The door closed behind them, and Jasmin felt a surge of triumph. Her plan had worked perfectly. Her father was safely away from Shanika, and all it had cost was a woman's dignity and trust. A small price to pay, she told herself, ignoring the uneasy feeling settling in her stomach.

In the car, David gripped the steering wheel tightly. "I can't believe it," he muttered, more to himself than to Jasmin.

"I'm sorry, Daddy," she said, her voice small. "I didn't want you to get hurt."

He reached over to squeeze her hand, his eyes still fixed on the road ahead. "You did the right thing, telling me."

Jasmin nodded and turned to look out the window, hiding the smile that threatened to break across her face.

Epilogue

Christmas morning dawned crisp and bright. Jasmin woke to the gentle murmur of voices from the living room—her mother's soft laugh, her father's deep chuckle. She lay still, wondering if she was dreaming.

It had all happened so quickly. Just two days ago, her father had updated his relationship status to "single." Shanika had gone silent on social media. The plan had worked, but Jasmin had worried that her father would be too heartbroken to celebrate Christmas with them. The voices from the living room proved otherwise.

She slipped out of bed and padded down the hallway, heart quickening with each step. When she rounded the corner, the sight before her seemed almost surreal: her parents standing side by side in matching Christmas sweaters, steaming mugs of hot cocoa in their hands, smiling beneath the twinkling lights of a perfectly decorated tree.

Her mother noticed her first. "Baby, put on your sweater!" Malia called out, gesturing to a red and green knit folded on the armchair. "This was a spur of the moment idea—we didn't do pajamas like we used to, but the sweaters will have to do for today."

Jasmin reached for the sweater with trembling hands, pulling it over her head. The wool was soft, the fit perfect. She looked up at her father, searching his face for signs of sadness or regret, but found only warmth in his eyes.

"Go ahead, baby girl," David encouraged, nodding toward the pile of brightly wrapped gifts beneath the tree. "Open your presents."

Jasmin approached the tree slowly, still feeling as though she might wake from this dream at any moment. She settled on the floor and reached for the first gift, peeling away the paper. As she moved from one present to the next, she caught her parents exchanging glances and smiles when they thought she wasn't looking.

The anxiety that had lived in her chest for months began to unravel. Her plan hadn't just worked; it had worked perfectly. Her family was whole again.

"How do you like your gifts?" Malia asked when the last box was opened.

In response, Jasmin launched herself into her mother's arms, then her father's. "This is the best Christmas ever!" she declared, and meant it.

David chuckled, reaching for his phone. "Come on, let me get a picture."

Jasmin posed by the tree, surrounded by her gifts, smiling so wide her cheeks hurt. David snapped several photos of her alone, then a few with Malia beside her. The camera captured their matching smiles, the contentment radiating between them.

"Wait a minute, now it's my turn!" Malia announced, taking the phone from David. She captured shots of Jasmin with her new presents, then a few of father and daughter together.

Seeing her opportunity, Jasmin spoke up. "Now we need one with all three of us!"

Her parents exchanged a brief glance before nodding in agreement. They huddled close together on the couch, Jasmin nestled between them as Malia extended her arm, angling her phone to fit them all in the frame.

"Say 'Merry Christmas!'" Malia instructed, tapping the screen once, twice, three times.

It was after the third photo that Jasmin saw it—a notification scrolling across the top of her mother's phone. A message from the game she played every night.

The game she played with SnakeEyes77.

Time seemed to stop. Jasmin's breath caught in her throat as the pieces suddenly clicked into place. Her father stood, oblivious, moving toward the kitchen to refill his cocoa.

"What is it?" Malia asked, noticing Jasmin's frozen expression.

Jasmin's gaze moved slowly from the phone to her mother's face, searching for confirmation of what she now suspected. "Nothing," she managed to say.

Malia held her daughter's gaze for a long moment, her expression unreadable. Then, slowly, her lips curved into a knowing smile.

"Ready for breakfast?" she called to David.

"Yes indeed!" came his cheerful reply from the kitchen, the sound of pans clattering following his words.

While David's attention was elsewhere, mother and daughter continued to stare at each other. Then, simultaneously, their lips curled into identical devious smiles. Malia's eyelid dropped in a subtle wink.

Jasmin felt a chill of recognition. All this time, she'd thought she was the master manipulator, the architect of her family's reunion. But now she understood—her mother had been playing the same game, working toward the same goal, guiding Jasmin's moves without her even realizing it.

As they moved to join David in the kitchen, Jasmin felt her mother's hand squeeze her shoulder.

The game was over. They had won.

Together.

The End

I hope you enjoyed this short Christmas story about such a precious little angel. Jasmin knew what needed to be done to get what she wanted for Christmas, and she acted accordingly.

What are your thoughts? I would love to hear from you. Share them in your review!

Want another thriller by me? Check out The Quiet Ones series – compared to Shonda Rhimes and Courtney A. Kemp! Each story is more twisty than the last. Check out the first book in the series, Should Have Thought Twice – on me :)

Watch out for the ***Quiet Ones****... You never know when they might snap.*

Until next time,

Before you go...

If you enjoyed *All I Want for Christmas is You*, I would absolutely love to hear your feedback. Please leave a **rating** or **review** commenting on your overall thoughts.

In addition, if you would like access to exclusive updates, giveaways, and more, join my email list at tanishastewartauthor.com/contact.

God bless you, and happy reading!

Tanisha Stewart

PS: If you would like to connect with me on social media, here's where you can find me:

Facebook: Tanisha Stewart, Author
Facebook group: Tanisha Stewart Readers
Instagram: tanishastewart_author
TikTok: authortanishastewart
Twitter: TStewart_Author
YouTube: Tanisha Stewart

Should Have Thought Twice: A Psychological Thriller

They say to always watch the quiet ones, because you never know when they might snap.

Shatina is a young woman with a troubled past and present. She lives in the shadows of her fraternal twin sister, who sucked up all the beauty genes, her best friend, whose seductive charm will sway any boy who listens, and her cousin, who is more than a knockout, but a force to be reckoned with.

Shatina feels like she has nothing going for her but her grades and her full scholarship to a four year institution of her choice... until someone comes along to threaten that.

Shatina has faced threats before, and little does anyone know, she has gained vindication over all of her enemies, one by one. Except this last one might be a bit more of a challenge than she bargained for.

Check it out here: Should Have Thought Twice: A Psychological Thriller

Every Voice Ain't From God: A Christian Romance Thriller

A psychological thriller with jaw-dropping twists and turns, and characters whose antics will leave you speechless... A story about love gone right, then wrong.

Zakari has known Nicole was **the one** since high school. He prays about whether their relationship is meant to be and receives confirmation one night during a church service. Zakari and Nicole are getting married!

Until **she breaks up with him** the next day.

Zakari plunges into a pit of despair, then Nicole reaches out and tells him they can be friends, maybe rekindle their relationship after college? Elated, Zakari agrees and bides his time until **he and Nicole can be together** again.

But Nicole gets **engaged to another man**, and Zakari doesn't understand.

He and Nicole are meant to be - she just needs to see it.

And **her fiancé needs to be eliminated**.

Every Voice Ain't From God is a twisted and page-turning tale about a man who will stop at nothing to have his woman's heart. **Including murder.**

Check it out here: Every Voice Ain't From God: A Christian Romance Thriller

Messed With The Wrong One: An Urban Romance Thriller

We all do things we live to regret, but when you harm the wrong ones, you get what you get.

Junior cheated. Marlena is furious. She resolves to teach him a lesson. What starts as a simple act of revenge, however, quickly takes a dangerous turn.

While Marlena was busy getting back at Junior, someone else happened to be planning a revenge of her own against Marlena. The deadly kind.

Marlena finds herself in a race against time to no longer change her man. Now she has to save him. And herself.

Check it out here: Messed With The Wrong One: An Urban Romance Thriller

The Governor's Wife

He was sent to do **one job**.

Get rid of the man the Governor's wife was sleeping with. A **single shot** was fired, and the mission should have been accomplished.

Instead, he shot the wrong person.

And now there's a **bounty on his head**.

The Governor's Wife is a fast-paced action thriller about a man who had one mission, but failed, and unbeknownst to him, that failed mission would unfold a whirlwind of conspiracies, secrets, and lies.

Check it out here: The Governor's Wife

Everybody Ain't Your Friend: An Urban Romance Thriller

They say you should keep your friends close, and enemies closer, but sometimes reality might be the other way around...

Mia thinks her life is completely normal. She has a loving boyfriend, great and supportive friends, and a close relationship with her mother.

Things take an interesting turn, however, when she is almost run down by a car one day. Then come the messages from an untraceable number. Not to mention the heartbreaking secret that is revealed shortly thereafter.

Suddenly, everything that Mia thought was right in her life goes wrong. She has no idea why, but she needs to find out, before her secret stalker decides her time is up.

Check it out here: Everybody Ain't Your Friend: An Urban Romance Thriller

Not What It Seems: A Christian Romance Thriller

Sparks begin to fly between Priscilla and Raheem, but soon they will learn, all is not what it seems.

Priscilla moves across the country to escape a toxic ex who won't let her go. Her mindset is healing, but within days of her arrival, she's introduced to the sexiest man she's ever laid eyes on: **Raheem.**

When Priscilla and Raheem's eyes meet, the chemistry is immediate. One would think they are a match made in heaven, and everything will go smoothly for them.

Wrong.

Because the closer Priscilla and Raheem get to one another, the more strange things begin to happen.

Sinister things.

What has Priscilla gotten herself into?

She's locked into Raheem, and he wants her to stay, but as the song goes, **jealousy is cruel as the grave...** (*Song of Solomon 8:6*).

Check it out here: Not What It Seems: A Christian Romance Thriller

Clean Up Woman

What happens when dreams turn deadly?

Yana is a **workaholic**. She has noble aspirations but isn't taking care of home. Meanwhile, **Sasha**, her new **nanny**, is more than ready to step in. Sasha and **Yana's husband**, Shawn, get closer, arousing suspicion by Yana.

But there's more to this nanny than meets the eye. More than what Yana bargained for.

Clean Up Woman is a **gripping suspense thriller** with jaw-dropping **twists and turns** you won't see coming.

Check it out here: Clean Up Woman

Caught Up With The 'Rona: An Urban Sci Fi Thriller

Cordell's luck could not be any worse. A young black man, a full-time student, doing his best to give back to his community by serving as a substitute teacher, only to receive an email which stated that his job would be suspended for the next three weeks due to the Coronavirus.

Frustrated about the situation, he vents to his lifelong friend, Jerone. Shortly after their conversation begins, they are approached by Markellis, a neighborhood hustler who always tries to sell Cordell and Jerone on his get-rich-quick schemes...

But this one is different. Cordell is pressed for cash, so he convinces Jerone to go along with Markellis' proposal.

No sooner than they say yes, Cordell and Jerone are swept up in an almost unspeakable conspiracy, with less than three weeks to turn it around...

Only it's much more than just Cordell and Jerone's lives that are at stake.

Check it out here: Caught Up With The 'Rona: An Urban Sci Fi Thriller

December 21st: An Urban Supernatural Suspense

Flick is a regular guy, living a regular life, then the night of Thanksgiving came.

It all started with a conversation he had with his cousin Bru that got a little heated.

Tensions rose, but things calmed down when he went to his mother's house for the family dinner.

Little did he know, that's when his life would begin to shift in a direction that he never expected.

December 21st, Saturn and Jupiter aligning, competing belief systems... what did it all mean?
Nothing, Flick thought.
Until the first event.
Then the second.

Follow Flick's journey in this Urban Supernatural Suspense as he tries to figure out exactly what's going on.

Is he losing his mind?

Or does everything that is happening have a deeper meaning?

Check it out here: December 21st: An Urban Supernatural Suspense

Where. Is. Haseem?! A Romantic-Suspense Comedy

Ever been ghosted??

Well, Stephanie has, and it doesn't feel good.

After a series of mishaps in the love department, Stephanie meets Haseem. They seem to hit it off and the chemistry between them is steadily building. Until...

Haseem disappears.

Where did he go??
No one seems to know.
But Stephanie is determined to find out.

Follow this story of romance, suspense, and comedy as Stephanie tries to figure out how the man of her dreams could just vanish without a trace.

Check it out here: Where. Is. Haseem?! A Romantic-Suspense Comedy

Tanisha Stewart's Thrillers

The Quiet Ones Series

Should Have Thought Twice: A Psychological Thriller

Fooled Me Once: A Psychological Thriller

Never Saw Me Coming: A Psychological Thriller

Reap What You Sow: A Psychological Thriller

Surprise Surprise: A Psychological Thriller

The Enemy You Know: A Psychological Thriller

The Love Conquers All Series

A Praying Wife vs A Preying Woman

A Praying Husband Versus A Preying Man

The Red Series

The Deadbeat: A Psychological Thriller

The Student: A Psychological Thriller

The Patient: A Psychological Thriller

The Bridesmaid: A Psychological Thriller

The Hitchhiker: A Psychological Thriller

The Babysitter: A Psychological Thriller

The Neighbor: A Psychological Thriller

The Trainer: A Psychological Thriller

The Dating App Horrors Series

The Perfect Profile, by Toni Larue'

Something About Kera, by Octavia Grant

Wish I Never Met Her, by Tanisha Stewart

Anything for Angel, by Kenya Moss-Dyme

The Deadliest Match, by Keira N. James

The Asylum Series

The Haunting Hour, by Toni Larue'

The Delinquent, by Tanisha Stewart

Mind Games, by Toni Larue'

The Journalist, by Tanisha Stewart

Standalones

Where. Is. Haseem?! A Romantic-Suspense Comedy

Caught Up With The 'Rona: An Urban Sci-Fi Thriller

December 21st: An Urban Supernatural Suspense

Everybody Ain't Your Friend: An Urban Romance Thriller

The Maintenance Man: A Twisted Urban Love Triangle Thriller

Not What It Seems: A Christian Romance Thriller

Vengeance Is Mine: A Psychological Thriller

Clean Up Woman

The Governor's Wife

In His Hands

Made in the USA
Middletown, DE
22 December 2025